i

Heart of a
Neighbor

Heart of a Neighbor

Book 2 of 3 of the:
American Neighborhood Series

by:
Lynn Hobbs

Dedication

This book is dedicated to my son and publisher, Jeff Brannon of Proof Publications; and to my granddaughter, Jessica Brannon.

Jeff; your patience of working countless hours with untimely interruptions has blessed us all. Your encouragement and Christian insight have been an inspiration to me. Thank you for making this book and this series possible.

Jessica; I'll always have fond memories of you helping with my edits. Thanks to you, there is no fist-bump, or Comanche war cry inside the story of this book. I enjoy and respect your God-given talent for writing, critiquing, and editing.

Much love to each of you, and my whole-hearted thanks; the time and efforts of both of you are greatly appreciated!

Chapter One

Richard, a master of manipulation, delighted in impressing others with the right word at the right moment. He used them to his advantage. He could lie, and steal without any remorse, and had tired of Lavinia.

He unlocked the front door and eased into the house. Making his way through the darkness, he reached Lavinia's bedroom. Cautious with each step, he approached the dresser.

She appeared to be asleep, and lay deathly still as she heard him rummage through her purse.

Richard's feet padded softly across the wooden floor. He exited the bedroom.

She strained to hear the front door open and shut, but only heard his shuffling feet move about various rooms. She remained rigid in bed, listening for the slightest movement inside or out of the house. Finally, he left. The confirming sound of the front door slamming brought a strange sensation of peace. Reluctant to move, she prayed.

Heavenly Father, I can't take him or his lies anymore. And I can't help him. I'm turning him over to You. He's in Your hands. I pray he comes to know You as his Savior.

As it did upon his arrival, Richard's car engine pierced the silence with a roar. He revved the motor, and let it idle before placing it in gear.

Lavinia, concentrating as the noise became subdued, mentally pictured the route he took departing the moonlit neighborhood. Relief flooded her being; he was indeed gone. Flinging the covers off her legs, she turned on the lamp, and spotted her purse. The contents lay helter-skelter across the top of the dresser. The billfold she'd hidden earlier in a closet shoebox lay on the floor open and empty. Her driver's license and other cards were thrown about the room.

"My rent money..." The words shot into the quiet room, and raced through her mind.

She scanned the closet. His clothes were gone. Bolting to the kitchen, she entered the pantry and groaned. No food.

Running her hand behind her neck, she sucked in the muggy, night air. A glance at the wall clock displayed 2:15 in the morning.

Busy man...

Annoyance surged as she noticed the 8x10 picture of Richard in the living room. The sly smile seemed to accentuate his overall sneaky appearance. "And I thought you'd changed, thought we could try one more time." Lavinia mumbled, snatching the picture frame. "Great way to start over." She pitched it in the trash can.

Gathering belongings, she packed her car. After writing her landlady a note about paying what she owed, Lavinia experienced the new calmness, again. Wide awake, she returned to her vehicle, her mind a whirlwind of activity.

Glad I didn't stop the divorce proceedings.

She remembered her attorney had admired her antique bracelet.

He wanted to buy it for his wife. Time to sell it and pay my landlady; never should have fallen behind with the rent, anyway. What happened then?

Her dark brows tangled in a scowl.

Oh, yes, Richard needed new boots. Way to go, Richard.

She pictured his flashing smile and the way he'd place his hand under her chin while he lied to her. Her face grew warm with shame, and she realized she already missed him.

But no more, I'm done.

She straightened her posture, and put the car in reverse.

Lavinia drove to her lawyers' office, parking under a street light near the front of the building. At 4 a.m. she drifted off to sleep.

Chapter Two

Kate Davis pulled into the handicap parking space full of energy until her feet hit the pavement. A blinding pain tore through her right knee. She grasped the car door handle, and waited for it to lessen. The pain subsided, and Kate limped to the sidewalk with mere throbbing.

She glanced at her surroundings and treasured being able to simply enjoy this day, even at a parking lot, and smiled.

Thank God I can stand, and thank God I can walk.

Vivid shades of rose, pink, violet, and yellow blended to form the dawning of the day. A gentle breeze lifted her hair, and Kate soaked in the morning.

Happy and determined, she continued to the back entrance of Christ Community Church. Volunteering in the kitchen each Friday proved to be as rewarding to her as to those she served. The free meal was well publicized and attendance was up from previous months.

The parking lot was usually vacant at this early hour, but today Kate noticed one vehicle in front of a nearby brick building.

Walking closer, she spotted someone sleeping stretched out on the front seat.

Not wanting to intrude, yet mindful of possibly being asked to identify this stranger, Kate focused on identification details. Turning to read the attorney's sign on the building, Kate dismissed the idea of foul play.

The stranger exhaled as if in a deep sleep. Kate left, and entered the church's kitchen.

Other volunteers arrived. Kate enjoyed the camaraderie as they slipped into their familiar routine. One hour had passed and breakfast was ready. Tables were set and aroma wafted from the church into the parking lot. Kate stood in front of huge pans of hot biscuits and watched as people entered. Pastor Williford blessed the food and reminded the crowd that another meal would be served at 5 pm.

Kate preferred working the breakfast meal.

Plates were grabbed and held as generous helpings were dished out to hungry people standing in line. Pleasant, Kate spoke to each one. Faces were worn and tired, yet everyone expressed their gratitude for the meal.

Most were seated when Kate glanced at the thinning line and looked directly into the sad eyes of the sleeping stranger from the parked car. Feeling drawn to the young woman, Kate left the food trays, and hurried to her. With a timid smile, Kate gave her a heartfelt hug, and patted her back.

The woman, not familiar with kindness, placed her hands over her face and cried.

Pastor Williford rushed to Kate's side and ushered the two women into his private office. Once seated, Kate offered her the box of tissues on Pastor Williford's desk, and he handed her a cold, bottle of water from the office mini kitchen.

She took what they gave her, and appeared lost. Her shoulders quivered as she sobbed. She drank a long gulp from the bottle, and her crying ceased. She blushed, and spoke in a hushed tone.

"Thanks. I don't even know your name."

"I'm Kate. Kate Davis."

"And I'm Lavinia, Lavinia Moore."

"Pastor Williford." The elderly man introduced himself with an extended hand. Lavinia gave him a warm handshake.

"I don't usually cry. I'm so embarrassed. I don't know what to say."

"You don't have to say anything." Pastor Williford unfurled his wrinkled brow.

Kate pivoted to the door. "Let me get you something to eat."

"Thank you, that would be nice, I uh, I don't always talk about my problems, but I feel I can trust you both."

"I was hoping you'd feel that way." Pastor Williford turned to Kate. "Bring her two plates."

"Oh no, just one." Lavinia laughed, and Kate sailed out the door.

"You and Kate are a lot alike. You don't like to talk about your problems, and Kate doesn't like to discuss her disability. She can't work a regular job."

"Oh?" Lavinia gave Pastor Williford her full attention.

"She knows I talk about it. She was rear-ended at a red light. Damaged her spine and had to have a total knee replacement on her right leg. Her lymph nodes were cut; slows her down a bit."

"Cut lymph nodes?"

"Causes swelling if she stays on her leg long. She's inspiring to us."

"How does she live with it?"

"Prayer and strong faith; I highly recommend both."

"My faith has been off focus for a while."

"Does the problem have a name?"

Lavinia's mouth fell open, and she sagged into the chair.

"Richard Moore."

"Your husband?"

"Yes, but not for long, Mr. Clyde Gorman is my attorney."

Pastor Williford nodded.

"I need to see him after I leave here."

"And after that? Where will you go?"

"Looking for work, I have good references for a secretary position."

"May I see your references?"

"Yes sir. Here is a copy." She handed him a typed page.

Pastor Williford scanned the information, and tucked it into his pocket. "What happened?"

"Richard came around. Things fell apart."

Kate entered the office carrying a tray piled high with dishes of scrambled eggs, biscuits, pancakes, and turkey sausage. She carefully placed the tray on Lavinia's lap.

Lavinia's eyes widened. "What a variety."

Kate sat next to her. "I mix honey and cinnamon on my biscuits." She motioned to the cinnamon shaker and squeeze bottle of honey. "Thought you might like it."

"Thanks."

Pastor Williford glanced at Kate as their guest starting eating. "Lavinia has secretary skills. I'll inquire if any of our members are in need of one."

"A few of them are business owners."

"I'll make some calls." He grabbed his cell phone and slipped out the door.

Kate's motherly instinct took control, and she looked at Lavinia with concern as one would look at a hurt child. Searching for ideas to remedy her situation, Kate was still at a loss, and leaned forward. "I'm glad you are here."

"Me too." Lavinia hesitated, and her voice softened. "I made drastic changes last night. I can't take the same stress over and over."

"Stress can make a strong person crumble, believe me, I know. We recently experienced a murder in our neighborhood. That was enough stress to last a lifetime. At least he was caught, and we can relax now."

"That had to be scary. Stress is destructive. We can't control what others do, or what may happen to alter our lives. I always think later of what I should have done. Maybe if I had said something different, things could have had a better outcome."

"We all consider that."

"My husband, Richard, can talk anyone into whatever would benefit him. I'd catch him at it, and accuse him of ulterior motives, and he'd turn it all around—try to make me feel guilty. He always blamed others if he didn't get hired; or if something was stolen. Never did take responsibility for his actions. Richard even made fun of me, and my Christian faith."

"I don't think it's God's will for you to be with Richard."

"I realize that now. I was so taken in by him, guess he brain-washed me."

"And here you are." Kate's eyes brightened.

"Yes. I was waiting for my lawyer's office to open and smelled the food. Then I remembered seeing the Free Food Friday posters in town."

Lavinia tipped her head back and groaned. "Richard stole my money, and my groceries last night; but everyone has stressful situations. How about you?"

Kate gazed down at her hands. "I lived in New Orleans when Hurricane Katrina hit. Lost everything." She stopped and made eye contact with Lavinia, then abruptly looked away. Her mouth tensed and words spilled out in a rapid pace. "What little family I had was never found, friends were scattered across shelters in nearby states, my home was destroyed…"

Lavinia sat motionless. "Oh Kate, I'm so sorry. I can't imagine living through all of that."

"I couldn't have made it without my faith."

Lavinia nodded. She remained quiet and seemed to struggle with what to say. After a few moments, she cleared her throat. "If you don't mind my asking, how did you end up here in Houston?"

"I inherited my Aunt's home, and it's such a blessing."

Pastor Williford entered his office taking long strides to his desk.

"You ladies getting acquainted?"

They exchanged a warm glance.

"Wonderful. Lavinia, you'll find we have a strong bond with each other. It begins with unity in Christ."

Lavinia gave him a curt nod.

He settled into his chair and handed her a hand-written page. "Here is someone interested in interviewing you. Dorothy Jones is the principal of our local elementary school. Your references checked out favorably as long as Richard stays away."

"Oh, that man is history, Pastor Williford. I can't thank you enough for an interview."

"You are welcome. Oh, one other thing young lady…"

"Sir?"

He handed her a key.

Lavinia shook her head. "I don't understand."

"We have a small furnished apartment adjacent to the parsonage. It's fully stocked. You are welcome to live there."

"Pastor Williford, you've got to be kidding." Lavinia glanced from Kate to the Pastor. "I don't know how to thank you."

"You can thank me by filling your mind with God's Word. That's how you'll get your strength back. Start by reading Isaiah 40:31."

"I will."

"Do you need gas money for this week?"

"No, I have a full tank."

"Okay, then your attorney's visit is next."

Lavinia, displaying a new confidence, stood erect so fast her chair scooted on the floor.

"I'll walk over there now."

Kate scribbled her home phone number on a sticky note pad from Pastor Williford's desk. "Here, keep in touch."

Lavinia snatched it heading for the door.

"I will. Thanks again."

She disappeared with a burst of energy leaving Kate and Pastor Williford to their own thoughts. They exchanged a brief glimpse at each other, and remained closemouthed. Kate fidgeted with her car keys and rose.

"Pray for her."

"Oh yes, Pastor. I will."

Kate returned to the breakfast serving line, but couldn't shake the forbidding mood that overcame her. Smiling her way through the next hour of clean up duties, she left, sinking into the front seat of her car where she prayed for Lavinia in earnest.

Chapter Three

The chattering of squirrels mingled with the distant sounds of chirping birds. Richard lay deep in the woods sprawled on damp soil. The sting of rain awoke him. Slapping at his face, he stood, weaving, trying to regain his balance. The effects of last night's meth were still present, and all sounds seemed foreign. Frowning, he made his way to the car. Stuck in the mud, it had served its purpose. He was no longer in Houston.

Hunger tore through his being, and he jerked the back passenger door open. Cans were scattered as if pitched into the vehicle. He reached for a can of tuna and starred at it.

A cold sweat popped out on his skin, and he had a sudden revelation.

No can opener.

Lavinia had his can opener.

He leaned the top portion of his body back, and emitted a lusty cry.

"Lavinia! I'm coming for you..."

His body shook as the illegal drugs forged through his veins.

The rain intensified.

Richard climbed into the front seat of the car, and passed out.

Chapter Four

Lavinia rushed up the stairs to Clyde Gorman's office suite. Opening the door, she was overwhelmed at the enormous expanse of empty space: 80 feet wide by 100 feet deep.

The only other time she'd seen it had given her the same experience. It was not expected then, and she would never get used to it. At that time, she didn't encounter any employees. Clyde Gorman greeted her from a side door in the room, discussed the uncontested divorce, set the court date, and Lavinia had paid the entire fee. Receipt in hand, she had left happy.

Today was different.

Mid way to the end of the room sat the receptionist behind a dark mahogany desk. Filing cabinets filled the space behind her. A few chairs were arranged on either side of the wall near her desk. The receptionist, about sixty years old with graying hair; raised her head, drew her mouth tightly together, and stared wide-eyed at Lavinia as if she had never seen a woman before.

Lavinia marched forward.

I've handled smug women before...

"May I help you?"

"Yes, I'm here to see Mr. Clyde Gorman."

"This is his late afternoon in court. He has no appointments today."

"He told me I didn't need an appointment."

"And you are?"

"Lavinia Moore."

"Well, Mrs. Moore, take a seat and when he comes out for lunch you may approach him. I will not disturb him."

"Fine. I'll wait."

Lavinia spotted the receptionist's name on a wooden plaque displayed in front of the desk; Julie Nugent.

And I can wait all day, Ms. Julie Nugent.

Lavinia selected a Texas Monthly magazine and found an article to read, then several other articles. Crossing her legs, she sat in a comfortable position, and read every article in four different magazines. At one time she yawned. Another time she caught the receptionist glaring at her, and Lavinia gave her a quick smile.

Two hours passed without either woman speaking. As the hands on the wall clock moved to eleven, a side door opened, and Clyde Gorman emerged.

Pulling his glasses down, he looked over the dark rims. "Mrs. Moore, is that you?"

"Yes, it's been awhile."

"Come in." He held the door, and she proceeded inside.

"Your divorce is almost final. In fact, it's scheduled for the first part of next week."

He sorted through a stack of folders on his desk, and removed one.

"Please be seated, I want to refresh my memory before I say anything further."

Lavinia eased into the closest chair.

Clyde Gorman studied page after page in the folder. After a brief nod at

Lavinia, he placed the pages back into the folder.

"Everything is in order. Meet me at 9 in the morning on Tuesday at the courthouse. Even if Richard doesn't show, it's a mere formality. Your divorce will be finalized."

"Great. Oh, and I brought my antique bracelet, if you still want it for your wife."

"Yes, I do want it. Are you sure about this?"

"Yes, it means nothing to me."

He reached in his billfold and handed Lavinia a few hundred dollar bills, and she gently placed the bracelet on his desk.

"A beauty. Thank you, Mrs. Moore."

"And I thank you, Mr. Gorman. See you Tuesday."

She ambled to the door, and he seemed mesmerized with the bracelet.

"Such intricate detail, yes, see you Tuesday." He glanced at Lavinia with a broad smile.

She let herself out, and her mouth fell open as she looked straight into the receptionist's face. The older woman fled from the door, and darted across the open room to her desk.

I can't believe it, eavesdropping; of all the nerve!

Lavinia hurried to her car and felt her blood pressure rise with each thought about the receptionist. Exhaling deeply, she dismissed their encounter.

Nope, you aren't going to ruin my day, lady. Lord forgive her.

And thank You, I can pay my rent now.

Lavinia zipped through the sparse traffic arriving at her landlady's house within minutes. She rang the doorbell, and an older woman peeped through the lace curtains.

Rushing outside, she hugged Lavinia. "Lavinia Moore, you are as good as your word." Betty Wakefield beamed.

"And I have your money." She counted the correct amount owed into Mrs. Wakefield's outstretched hands, who in turn crammed it in her pocket. She wrote a receipt, giving it to Lavinia with a bowing gesture.

"Oh, please, Mrs. Wakefield, no need for that." Lavinia's face flushed a light shade of crimson. "I was behind, remember?"

"Yes, but you said you'd pay today, and you did. Makes me happy, unlike some people we both know."

"Who are you referring to? What happened?"

"What didn't happen, you mean. A police detective came this morning looking for Richard Moore."

"Did he say why?"

"No, and I let him look inside your apartment. He found Richards picture in the trash can and took it. I didn't think you'd care to have it."

"No ma'am."

"Detective Marino was his name. He gave me his card and told me to call him if Richard ever comes back."

"Yes ma'am. Well, with me gone he shouldn't return. Hope you find someone to rent the apartment, soon."

"Thank you, and Lavinia; be careful."

"I will, and you too, Mrs. Wakefield."

Lavinia slipped into her car and drove off. The instant she reached the stop sign, a loud thud exploded under her car. Turning off the ignition, she jumped out. Smoke engulfed the car. Walking on wobbly legs, she bent to examine the underside of the vehicle.

Thank God I don't see flames, or a flat tire.

Choking, she shuffled away. The smoke stunk, and billowed.

"Ma'am, are you okay?"

Lavinia jerked her head, and saw a tall biker with a black bandanna tied around the top of his head. She turned and noticed his parked motorcycle under a carport.

"Yes, uh, thank you."

"I don't mean to frighten you, ma'am. I live here. Saw your car smoking. Let me take a look." He crawled under the car for a closer inspection, and finally squirmed out, towering over Lavinia.

"Someone's playing a joke on you, ma'am. That is a smoke bomb. Kids prank each other with them all the time."

"Are you sure it's safe to drive?"

"It's harmless. Here, I'll start it up for you."

He scooted into the car and turned on the ignition. The car sounded normal.

"Thank you."

"No problem, ma'am."

He ambled to his lawn, and Lavinia coughed in spurts. The stench of old motor oil from the smoke bomb combined with the smell of smoke, and lingered like a toxic low lying cloud in the air.

No problem, indeed.

Driving back to her new apartment, the car began acting sluggish. Frowning, Lavinia tried to accelerate only to have the vehicle slow itself. She pulled off the road again. Cracking her knuckles, she muttered under her breath. Reaching for her cell phone, she poked at 9-1-1.

"9-1-1, what is your emergency?"

"Someone has vandalized my car. Is it possible for me to speak to a Detective Marino?"

"One moment while I transfer."

Lavinia's nostrils flared while she waited.

"Detective Marino here."

"Are you the one searching for Richard Moore today?"

"Yes ma'am. Do you know where he is?"

"No, but I know where he's been. I'd like to talk to you."

"I'll be right there. Where are you?"

"I'm in the 3000 block of E. 19th Street. My Toyota Rav 4 is on the side of the road. You can't miss it. It's the one still smoking from a smoke bomb."

"I'm on my way."

Chapter Five

Large rain drops splattered her windshield, and Lavinia flinched as lightening flashed.

Great timing...

She sprang from the smoking vehicle the instant the police car arrived. A plain clothed officer exited the vehicle and approached her.

"Mrs. Moore?"

"Yes."

"Detective Marino. Let's talk in here." He escorted her to the passenger side of his car, and she climbed inside. Rain escalated as he dashed around the front of the car, and slid inside behind the steering wheel.

He handed her a box of tissues, and they each dried their wet face and arms.

"I'm calling the fire department for your car." He yelled over the deafening rain.

"The brakes went out, and I was told the smoke was from a prank smoke bomb."

"I'm not allowed to search your vehicle without your permission. Do I have your permission?"

"Yes, please."

He called for help. The fire department found nothing. The police investigation resulted in her car being impounded.

He called in a request for a wrecker to dispatch.

"Now, we wait, again." He pivoted in the seat and faced her. "I'll need your car keys when the wrecker gets here."

Lavinia fumbled with the key ring and finally removed one key. Handing it to him, she grimaced.

"Thanks, Mrs. Moore. Now what's this all about?"

"My husband is Richard Moore. We're getting a divorce." She paused, reeling back at the sudden flashing lights penetrating through the heavy downpour. "That was fast."

Detective Marino glanced at the wrecker, and sprang from his patrol car. Lavinia watched him run to it, and give the key to the driver. He whirled his hands about as if explaining something, and drenched, hurried back to his patrol car.

"Let's talk at headquarters, and get out of this rain."

Lavinia heard him over the deluge, and nodded.

At the police station, Lavinia sank into the padded, leather love seat at Detective Marino's office. Over coffee, she gave him her address, driver's license number, and date of birth. He refilled her coffee, and feeling at ease, she informed him of the previous night's encounter with Richard.

"He terrifies me. I don't want to upset him with confrontations, but I do want my divorce."

"I understand, Mrs. Moore, nonetheless, your safety is our priority.

I'd like to send some of our team to your new apartment to check it out. Make sure it really is safe."

"I haven't moved in, yet. My belongings are in my car."

"Oh. Then you really do need your car..."

With a look of resignation on her face, Lavinia said, "I'm trying to start over."

"I understand." Detective settled into his overstuffed swivel chair.

"Richard may be tied to illegal drug activity. Has he had any phone calls late at night?"

"He used too, but he moved out weeks ago."

"Any new friends?"

"I don't know."

"Why would he damage your car?"

"He's been acting strange, kind of distant, and then he gets loud and angry. I just don't trust him anymore."

"We may have to keep your car for evidence, if we can prove he sabotaged it."

Lavinia lowered her head gazing at the floor.

"Mrs. Moore, you are not defeated. You are in good hands."

"I know. I'm thinking about work, getting to work."

"First things first, I am issuing a warrant for Richards arrest in the robbery at your old apartment. We had stopped patrolling your neighborhood, but will resume surveillance strictly on your new apartment."

"Thanks, but why were you patrolling?"

"Unfortunately, a murder happened a few months ago, but the assailant was indicted. Continued surveillance was a precaution, and no other criminal activity happened." He leaned forward in his chair. "We will patrol until Richard is apprehended."

"Thank you."

"I'll need you to write any information about him you can think of. His last job, his friends, his family, their names and addresses, make and model of his car, and what color it is." He handed her a spiral notebook, and a pencil.

Lavinia filled an entire page in minutes and flipped over to a new one. Writing in silence, she forgot about her coffee, and after hesitating at times, finished with three full pages.

She rose and plopped the notebook onto the Detective's desk. A wet, stray curl fell over the side of her face and she blushed, sliding it behind her ear.

Detective Marino beamed.

"Mrs. Moore, I've never enjoyed meeting anyone more than meeting you in the rain today."

Lavinia laughed, noticing the sopping wet areas splattered over his clothes.

"I'll drive you home now, if you're ready."

"Thanks, I am."

He handed her his business card as they exited the office.

"Don't hesitate to call."

Lavinia, confident again, walked with perfect posture, and a half smile spread across her face.

Chapter Six

Kate stepped into the alley behind her house, and filled her trash receptacle. Securing the lid, she paused, listening to unfamiliar voices coming from next door. A child cried in agony as muffled conversations grew; one soft and comforting, the other firm and clearly in control of whatever the situation demanded.

Returning inside her home, she retrieved the taco casserole she'd made for Lavinia and headed out to the car.

A white U-Haul truck plastered with gaily colored advertising had backed into the drive way next door. A middle aged man pushed a stack of boxes on a dolly and wheeled it to the open garage. A woman, short with long

dark hair, carried a little girl who must
have had her sleep disturbed —arms and
legs dangled as the child wailed. A
young boy brought up the rear.

Kate gazed at the new neighbors
with admiration.

What a sweet family...

Placing the casserole on the floor
board in her car, she hurried across the
lawn.

The man exited the garage with an
empty dolly, and at first didn't notice
her.

"Welcome to the neighborhood, I
live next door." Kate called out.

Weary, but smiling faces greeted
her as she approached.

All activity stopped. The man was
closer to her, and the woman turned
from entering the house. Both stared.

"I'm Kate Davis." She extended her hand to the man. He responded with a vigorous handshake while making eye contact.

"Sal Hernandez, and my wife, Maria." He pointed to Maria with a flourish of his arm. "And children; Rosa and Carlos."

Maria beamed.

"Can I help you with anything? Unloading the truck, or sitting with the children?"

"Oh no, thank you. We've traveled all night, and are ready to rest."

Kate nodded at Sal.

"Then let me bring you lunch today."

"How thoughtful. Yes, we would appreciate lunch." Maria said. Still carrying their daughter, she shifted the child to her other hip. Rosa clutched Maria's shoulder, and Maria muttered something to the sleepy child.

"I'll be back around noon." Kate sensed their need to be left alone, and hurried back to her property.

Climbing into her car, she thought again of her own family. They'd been separated across town when Hurricane Katrina hit New Orleans. It had been twelve years ago, and even now, it was a constant struggle not to yearn for them. She prayed their death had not been painful. Memories of being isolated in the attic returned as if the ordeal had just happened. Alone, she had fought panic and fear by praying as each foot of water rose inside the family home.

Rescued days later, she joined hundreds of other flood victims searching for family members who would be listed forever as missing. And she joined hundreds now dealing with a nervous stomach in each hurricane season, but it wasn't as bad as it had once been.

Trying to block the sadness, Kate drove off toward Lavinia's apartment, and turned on the radio. A lively instrumental filled the car, and Kate felt her mood lighten. She pictured herself as a young girl riding on top of her daddy's shoulders, happily joining in with a marching jazz parade shuffling down Bourbon Street. Kate smiled to herself remembering her shrill, childish laughter, and his deep belly laugh could be heard above the music.

Daddy was strict, but spontaneous; fun times.

Putting her family memories away as if tucking them into a safe place inside her heart, Kate focused on her day.

She drove by the parsonage and didn't see Lavinia's car behind it at the apartment. Circling to the front, she spotted Pastor Williford setting his trashcan on the curb, and lowered her window.

"Good morning."

"Good morning to you. Looking for our girl?"

"I was. I should have got her phone number."

"Wouldn't have helped today."

Kate squinted. "Why?"

"She's been at the police station."

"What? Lavinia?"

"Uh-huh. She called; all she said was a Detective was bringing her home."

"Well, I don't know what happened, Pastor, but my gut feeling tells me she's good people."

"And if she's not?"

"God placed her in our path."

"Exactly. She needs our help, Kate, regardless."

"I was surprising her with a casserole."

"What did you make?"

"Taco casserole."

"She'll love it. Got it in the car?"

"I do."

"I'll give it to her for you."

A sly smile crept over Kate's face. "Maybe she'll share."

"Maybe." He chuckled.

"It's in the back."

Pastor Williford opened the back passenger door and retrieved the covered dish. Slamming it shut, he frowned. "She should be coming home soon."

"I'll let you know if I hear anything."

"Same here." He stepped back from her car.

Kate shifted into drive and eased away from the curb.

Lavinia's doing what I did, starting over with strangers. She must feel totally alone.

Maneuvering through traffic, Kate spotted an blue neon sign blinking 'open' at a coffee shop. It loomed ahead, and Kate changed lanes in time to make the exit. Racing to the drive through lane, she ordered a caramel latte, and considered what to bring the Hernandez family for lunch.

Already 11:00, no time to cook. Looks like it's a Popeye's Fried Chicken day.

She pulled back into traffic and made her way to the fast food restaurant. The jingle, 'Love That Chicken at Popeye's' kept playing over and over in her mind. Driving through their parking lot, she got a heavy whiff of the fried chicken, and the delicious aroma of Louisiana Cajun food made her mouth water.

Yep, it's going to be a fried chicken kind of day for all of us.

Chapter Seven

Lavinia waved to Detective Marino, and watched him drive away. A quick scan of the neighborhood assured her all seemed normal.

Pastor Williford leaned out the door of the parsonage.

"I don't see your car. You okay?"

"Yes sir. Thank you. It's being checked out. The police wanted information about Richard."

"If I can help, let me know. Oh, I almost forgot; Kate came by earlier and left something for you. I'll get it."

The older gentleman returned carrying the covered dish with both hands. Lavinia stepped closer and raised her eyebrows.

"Take the lid off."

Lavinia snatched the cover and gazed at the baked delight.

"Oh my…"

"It's taco casserole."

"How thoughtful, but this is too much for me. Come on, help me eat it."

"I won't turn that down. Kate makes the best one I've ever had."

"Sounds great. A home cooked meal, new friends, and a new apartment I haven't seen yet. Maybe you can show me the apartment before we eat."

"My pleasure."

They meandered over the lawn to the apartment, and entered the home.

"Do you have any family living nearby? Any children?"

"No, Lavinia, they live in other states. We keep in touch though, and I have my church family. What about you?"

"My parents live in Rosenberg, and I have a sister in Brenham."

"And I have grandchildren your age." He swerved, catching his balance. "Guess I need to use that cane again. Maybe this time I'll try the walker. It has a seat."

"Can I get it for you?"

"No, that's okay. I think I'll get it out of the closet this afternoon." He smiled.

Lavinia's eyes brightened, and she considered him with fondness.

And I think I've just secretly adopted me a grandfather...

She followed him to the kitchen. He set the food on the counter, and walked her through each room.

"I like the reading nook in the small library." Lavinia opened cabinets, and grabbed two plates. "And this kitchen is enormous."

"The place is larger than you'd think." Pastor Williford filled his plate and set it in the microwave.

Lavinia discovered ice cold bottles of water in the refrigerator, and retrieved them while the Pastor added silverware to their place settings. The buzzer sounded to remove the first plate, and he snatched his plate out as Lavinia hurried to heat her portion of taco casserole.

They continued in a fast pace until they bumped into each other.

"You'd think we were starving." Lavinia chuckled.

"I think we are." The Pastor laughed.

They pulled their chairs out from the table in a swift motion, and sat.

Lavinia glanced at the Pastor, and he bowed his head.

"Heavenly Father, we thank You for this day, and this meal. Bless the hands that prepared it, and nourish it for our bodies. In Jesus name we pray, Amen."

"Amen."

The spicy scents from the taco casserole filled the room as both enjoyed several mouthfuls.

"Umm, this is delicious." Lavinia took another bite as melted cheese dripped into long strings hanging from her fork.

"Kate loves to cook, and she's good at it. Her dishes are the first to empty at our eating meetings."

"Eating meetings?"

"Once a month we meet and eat together. Everyone brings something; always great fellowship, and great food. You'll have to come. It's the last Sunday of each month at 6 o'clock in the evening."

"I will. I'll look forward to it."

"You'll like our church family. They are just themselves; a good, caring group."

"And not one is pretentious?"

"Not here. We even had a wedding this past winter. A widower, Daniel Star, married a newcomer, widow by the name of T9C Walker. One of the nicest weddings I've officiated, and the wedding cake was light and moist. The highlight was Daniel's young daughter, Aleesha, who sings solo. She does our special music on Sunday mornings. Sings like an angel, and she sang at their wedding. They make a wonderful family."

"Well, that's encouraging, good people are still around."

"Yes ma'am. Sometimes they run into a problem, and we help them along."

Lavinia looked in the kind eyes of the older Pastor. "I know in my case, you can't make someone love you, or make someone have compassion for others."

"Lives can be changed when people want to change. And when they have a good example to follow."

"You're right."

The shrill ringing of his cell phone interrupted their discussion.

He glanced at his caller I.D. and then at Lavinia. "Excuse me. It's Kate."

"Tell her I love the taco casserole, and thanks."

He nodded. "Hello? Where am I? Ha, I'm eating lunch with Lavinia, and we both love your food. She said to tell you thanks."

He fidgeted with his napkin as he listened to Kate.

"I'll ask her." He held the phone down and raised his head toward Lavinia. "Kate wants to visit you this afternoon."

"Sure. I'll be here."

"Kate, that will work. What? You are taking fried chicken to the

Hernandez family? I don't believe I've met them."

He paused, giving his full attention to Kate.

"Okay, you can tell me later. By."

He slipped his phone back into his pocket. "She'll be here around three o'clock. She's taking fried chicken to some new neighbors."

"I keep hearing about food when you and your church members are mentioned."

"It's part of fellowship. We're old-fashioned that way."

"I like old-fashioned. Here, let's split the rest of this." Lavinia sprang from her chair.

"What? I get more?"

"Yes. Ah, these will do." She found deep, plastic containers with lids and spooned the remainder of the casserole into them.

"We can freeze these for another day." Handing him two, she settled back into her chair. "Thank you for everything. I feel at home."

"You are mighty welcome, glad you are here. I'm a firm believer that God had this place ready for you. I give Him the credit."

"I agree."

Chapter Eight:

Henry shoved thick, white hair off his forehead and squinted at the parked vehicle. It was thirty yards from the road surrounded in high grass. Killing the engine, he hopped off his orange Kabota tractor, and approached the parked car with caution. His dog followed a few yards behind. Its low growl grew to guard dog madness the closer he advanced. Teeth barred, he leaped at the car barking at the sleeping face against the inside window.

"Hush, Cletus. Stop."

Henry watched the man stretch and sit upright in the seat. Upon seeing Cletus nearby, the blank expression on the man's face turned into wide-eyed alarm.

"It's okay, Buddy. I'm here to help." Henry waved at the stranger.

The window lowered as an extended arm shot out. The men shook hands, and Cletus growled in agitation.

"Henry Greenberg."

"Richard Moore."

"How long you been stuck?"

"Sometime after the rain. I was going too fast in that curve. Started sliding off the road, and landed in the mud."

"You okay?"

"Yeah, sore from sleeping here all night."

Henry nodded. "I'll pull you out with my tractor."

"I do appreciate it, sir."

"You don't have to call me sir. I'm Henry."

"Well, sir, uh Henry; I was taught to respect my elders, and I certainly am proud you came along this morning."

"Thank you, young man. Now put your car in gear."

Richard frowned. "In gear?"

"Put the car in neutral, so I can pull it."

"Yes sir."

Henry placed his tractor on the road behind the car, and attached a long chain to the undercarriage of the vehicle. Tires spun, and the motor strained as he maneuvered the car out of the high grass and mud. Pulling it slow, he managed to drag the car onto the road.

The dog had found a new interest in pawing at something in the weeds.

Richard ignored the now docile animal, left the car, and untied the chain. He helped Henry weave it through a metal rack behind the tractor seat.

"Richard, come have breakfast with us."

"Thank you, I'll take you up on that."

Henry drove the tractor with Cletus trotting alongside. Richard drove the mud-splattered car as careful as if it were brand new. He sat straight in the front seat with both hands on the wheel traveling about twenty miles an hour.

Henry glanced in his rear view mirror and mumbled to himself. "Seems like such a polite young man, wonder where he's from?"

They drove a few miles before turning into Henry's driveway. The home was positioned far from the road, surrounded in a cluster of tall, pine trees. The long ranch style house with an equally long porch was complete with a row of traditional wooden rocking chairs handmade in Texas. Painted white, they were heavy and oversized with high backs. A woman sat in a wheel chair watching the two men through binoculars.

Richard scanned the elaborate area and ran his hand through his disheveled hair. They parked and ambled toward the wide, concrete sidewalk leading to the home.

"Wilma, we have company. I invited him for breakfast."

She sat the binoculars on the side table and wheeled herself closer to greet them. "Welcome. Hope you're hungry."

They walked onto the porch and Henry completed introductions. "Richard, this is my wife, Wilma. Wilma, Richard Moore."

"Nice to meet you, Richard."

"Same here, ma'am, and yes, I am hungry."

"I found him with his car stuck in the weeds a few miles back, been there all night."

"That was a long, rainy night. Come inside."

Wilma led them down a hallway. "Cook has everything ready. We always eat when Henry returns from checking the fences. You can clean up in here."

She motioned to a door and both men entered.

Wilma wheeled herself to the huge kitchen. Aroma lingered in the room, and she smiled at the woman wearing an apron.

"Smells like homemade yeast rolls again. Thank you so much. Oh, we need another place setting. Henry has brought someone home."

A middle aged woman nodded and bustled about the kitchen gathering more eating utensils. Food was placed family style on the mahogany table along with pitchers of orange juice, water, and a carafe of coffee.

Henry and Richard arrived, both sitting and viewing the food in each platter and bowl.

Wilma positioned herself beside Henry.

He lowered his head and prayed. "Dear Lord, Thank You for this day, for Your blessings, and for this meal, and forgive us where we have failed You. In Jesus name we pray, Amen."

"Amen." Wilma and Richard both spoke in unison.

"Help yourself, Richard. We pass everything to each other. Don't be shy."

"Uh, no sir. I'm not shy with food."

Plates were filled with a variety of eggs, meats, fruit, and fresh rolls. In between bites, Wilma addressed the visitor.

"I don't believe I've seen you before."

"No ma'am. I'm from Houston. Where are we at anyway?"

"Not far from Houston. This is Shepherd, Texas. We live close to the Sam Houston National Forest."

"Well, I sure thank you for your hospitality. I'll head on back home right after breakfast. This is so kind of you, and you too, Henry."

"You're welcome. Want some more coffee?"

"Yes, please."

They finished the meal, and Richard rose.

"May I use your restroom before I go?"

"Yes, of course. You know where it is." Henry motioned down the hall.

Richard stepped lightly, and could still hear the couple talking as he entered the restroom.

He rushed to the medicine cabinet, and flung the door open. Green prescription bottles of pain pills lined the top two shelves. He dropped all of the bottles into his pants pockets, and closed the medicine cabinet "Like robbing a sitting duck. Yes sir." He mumbled to himself. "I always respect my elders. They keep pain pills in their bathrooms."

Grinning, Richard sauntered into the kitchen.

"Thanks again for all your help."

"Oh, don't leave so soon. Sit out on the front porch with us."

"I can't ma'am, I need to go, but I'll wheel you out there."

"She's independent, Richard, won't let anyone push her." Henry shook his head at his wife. "But let's go outside, we'll see you off."

Wilma beamed, and forged ahead. The men followed and stood in the warm sunshine.

"I can't thank both of you enough." Richard smiled, and shook Henry's hand.

"Glad to help. Take care, Richard."

They watched him drive away, and Henry glanced at Wilma.

"I forgot about the dried mud on his car."

"He didn't seem too concerned about it, but he sure did thank us a lot."

"And he sure was in a hurry to leave." Henry faced his wife. "I think

I'll have another cup of coffee." He held the front door open. "Coming in?"

"Yes, I forgot to take my morning pills." Wilma wheeled into the house, and both headed to the kitchen. She opened a drawer near the sink and glanced at the weekly pill dispenser. Henry handed her a glass of water, and poured himself a cup of coffee.

"I'm going into town later. Do you need to refill any of your prescriptions?"

"No. I hadn't opened the 90 day supplies yet."

She pulled the pharmacy's white paper bag from the back of the drawer. The receipt was still stapled to the top. Ripping it open, she cut her finger on the staples edge.

"Ouch." Wilma thumbed through the paper bag. "Yep, they are all here."

Blood oozed down her hand, and she wiped it on the bag.

"Here's a paper towel. I'll go get the Band-Aids." Henry took off to the bathroom.

He opened the medicine cabinet and saw the top two shelves were empty. He took several Band-Aids from a box, and returned to the kitchen laughing.

"What is it?" Wilma held her finger under a stream of water. Henry grabbed her finger, and dabbed a paper towel over it.

"You remember those hydrocodone bottles in the medicine cabinet?"

"Of course, I do." She flinched as he applied two Band-Aids to her finger. "The kids used them in that play at school. I think it was called 'Say No to Drugs.' Was that it?"

"That's the one."

Wilma nodded. "The pill bottles were filled with sugar pills."

"Well, they're all gone."

Chapter Nine

Kate bought a gallon of sweet tea for the new Hernandez neighbors, and a gallon of fruit punch for their children. She exited the grocery store and managed to arrive at the Hernandez home at a quarter to noon. Placing the box of fried chicken, and the drinks on a bench near their front door, Kate rang the doorbell.

At first, stillness greeted her. She rang the doorbell again. The front door opened, and a young boy stared at her.

"Un momento por favor."

He ran off inside the house. She waited as heavy footsteps approached.

Sal flung the door wide open, and seemed happy to see her.

"Kate, thank you for returning."
He spied the food on the bench. "And
for your kindness. My wife and
daughter are still asleep."

"Don't disturb them. Enjoy the
food, and welcome to the
neighborhood."

"Thank you. Maybe we can help
you someday."

She nodded, and turned to leave.
The little boy lifted the closed top on the
box of fried chicken and quickly tugged
at her shirttail.

"Muchas gracias." He placed his
arms around her leg, and gave her a
quick hug.

"You are welcome." Kate smiled
at the happy child.

He and his father both beamed, and Kate, touched by the boy's tenderness, left in a joyous mood.

She drove the short distance to her own home. Taking her smaller box of fried chicken to the kitchen counter, she grabbed a bottle of water, and devoured the meal.

She still had hours to kill before going to Lavinia's.

Turning on the television in the living room, she sank into the recliner elevating her legs to enjoy her quiet time. Watching the news channel was another daily enjoyment. She didn't always agree with the announcer's opinions, or what was happening across the nation, but she was informed.

A truck commercial came on featuring a merry jingle about a father and son. Kate stopped and watched the father return home with a miniature version of his own truck for the boy to drive.

How cute, reminds me of the sweet little Hernandez boy and his quick smile. Hmm, wonder why he only spoke Spanish and not English? None of my business...

Kate felt drowsy when sudden, dramatic music emitted loudly from the television. Recognizing the theme of breaking news, she sat upright. The words Breaking News were flashed in time with the pounding music. Kate absentmindedly twisted a ring on her index finger waiting for the announcer to appear on live television. The music stopped as a woman dashed to the news desk. Kate leaned forward.

"This is Jackie Wallace with your Houston Metro News. It has been confirmed that the body of local resident, Becky Meyers, wife of Ethan Meyers was discovered in a vacant field near the George Bush Intercontinental Airport. Due to the ongoing investigation, authorities are not releasing further information but homicide is suspected. The public is urged to call the Houston Police Department if you have any information; anonymity will be guaranteed."

A picture of Becky with a brilliant smile filled the screen, and Kate's stomach knotted into tiny, hard pieces.

Becky, oh no, not Becky...

Kate forgot to breathe. With a sudden, deep inhale, she remembered her nervous stomach as it convulsed.

She turned off the television knowing the attempt wouldn't calm her.

She was my neighbor, my friend...

Her phone rang. Kate snatched at it speaking in a shaky voice.

"Hello?"

"Kate, this is Pastor Williford."

"Pastor, I just saw Becky's picture on the news."

"I did too. Horrible. I feel so sorry for her, and her husband."

"I can't stand the thought of homicide. Poor Becky. I hope she wasn't killed. Did Steve kill her? She sure trusted him. What happened? Does anyone know what happened?" Kate pleaded.

"I don't know. Ethan is in the hospital. He's in therapy from a bad fall. Twisted something. Anyway, he said Becky never returned after leaving with Steve, never even phoned."

"I don't understand how she could do that. And Ethan is in the hospital?"

"Right here in Herman Hospital. He called me two days ago. I went to see him. He is making progress."

"Pastor, you know Steve is Becky's half-brother. What you don't know is Steve said when they lived in Kansas Ethan was a Peeping Tom. And Ethan told me Steve was after his half-sister's inheritance. He said Steve had stalked Becky before she knew he was her half-brother."

"And you think...?"

"I think Steve was sneaky, and trying to discredit Ethan. I lived across the street from Ethan and Becky, and Ethan did everything for her. Ethan seemed to be a wonderful husband to Becky, and she never helped him with anything. She did not deserve Ethan. Steve had motive to kill Becky, not Ethan."

"Ethan couldn't if he wanted to; he's been in the hospital for a week. You have strong opinions, and I know you are not judging."

"No, I am not. Just stating the facts I know are true."

"Why don't you call Ethan?"

"Pastor, he is a married man."

"No, Kate, not anymore." He paused. "Didn't you notice he wasn't home across the street?"

"No, I knew Becky left with Steve against Ethan's wishes, but he was still a married man who loved his wife. His coming and going was none of my business."

"They were both your friends, I don't think you should avoid him."

"Okay, Pastor, I will call him, and offer my condolences."

"As a fellow church member, he deserves that. You are his neighbor, Kate. You're familiar with him and Becky on a daily basis. I'm going back to visit him in person. If I can help him in any way, I will."

"Me, too. Ethan is a good man. He's never done anything questionable to me. He even bought a friend of mine her groceries, and she was leery of him because he winked at her after he paid her grocery bill. That's his way; he winks to be friendly, not any other reason."

"And Becky?"

"Becky was my friendly neighbor. I enjoyed our talks. I may not like how she treated Ethan, but her life was too short. She should still be alive and busy. I suspect Steve was involved in her death, and he will inherit everything from their family."

"Well, we have no evidence, and we both know assumptions and guesses are just that, stories with no facts. Do call Ethan."

"I am. I have to think about all of this. Let's talk later."

"Okay, and pray about it. I will. By."

"I'll pray, too. By."

Kate gazed at the phone. Her mind whirled. She thought of poor Becky.

Was she traumatized before her death? If she had an attacker, did she know that person? Was it Steve? And poor Ethan. I'm sure he is grieving. Probably can't even eat. And me, what an awful neighbor I've been. Do I tell him I didn't miss seeing him across the street? That I didn't know he wasn't even home, much less in the hospital?

Kate cringed at making the phone call to Ethan.

I haven't been a good neighbor to him, but I couldn't, he was a married man. That would have been improper, against my principles. Lord, I pray for Your guidance and Your will in my life and I pray to be a light as a witness for

You to Ethan, and not an intrusion. In
Jesus name I pray, Amen.

Kate found the phone number for
the hospital, and called it.

"Hermann Hospital."

"Could you ring the room that
Ethan Myers is in?"

"Yes ma'am."

The operator clicked off, and a
phone began ringing.

Ethan's weary voice answered.

"Hello?"

"Ethan? This is Kate."

"Oh, Kate!" Ethan sobbed into the
phone.

Kate put her hand over her mouth
and felt his pain. He cried in anguish,
and for the first time, she couldn't. She
realized Ethan needed a friend, and she
waited for him to compose himself.

However long it took, she would wait for him to cry it out.

Thank you, Lord, for guiding me to call him…

Ethan spoke first.

"Kate, she's been gone for months and never called. Not once. I know Steve was after her money. I know it, but I don't know how she died. I can't say it was done by Steve. All I know is they're doing an autopsy; don't know when the funeral can be scheduled."

"I'm so sorry this happened to her and to you."

"They were living in Galveston on the beach."

"Are there any suspects?"

"Steve is a person of interest, that's all the police told me."

"Ethan, it's so hard to comprehend. And how did you get in the hospital? I had no idea you weren't at home."

"I've been here for a week. Fell down the stairs in the cellar. Twisted my ankle, and it's swollen; pulled some leg muscles, but I'm on the mends now. Should be able to go home soon."

"If I can help with anything, let me know."

"Well, there is one thing." He paused.

"What Ethan?"

"Mine and Becky's dog. Steve might not take care of it, and he may even get arrested, I don't know what will happen, but I want our dog back. Rufus has to be confused with Becky gone." His voice quivered at the mention of Becky.

"Where is the dog?"

"I have the address in Galveston. Steve has his own dog. He can't object to me getting Rufus back."

"Tell you what, you contact the police, clear the way for me, and I'll go get your dog."

"Kate, would you do that? I can make the arrangements for tomorrow or the next day, if it's okay with you. All you have to do is drive and pick him up. I'll even pay for the gas."

"I can go anytime, but no, you are not paying for the gas. Make the arrangements, and call me when it's okay to get Rufus."

"Okay."

"You try to get some rest, Ethan, and I'll be praying for you."

"Thanks, Kate. By."

"By, Ethan." Relieved the call was over, Kate noticed her hand shook as she laid the phone down. Panic spread through her body. "This is ridiculous. I was only talking to Ethan."

Uttering a prayer, she left the house, and drove to Lavinia's. Kate felt a sudden calmness thinking about the poor dog. Arriving at her destination, she banged on Lavinia's door.

Lavinia opened it fast. "Hi, lady." She grinned.

"Hi, yourself. What are you doing tomorrow?"

"My divorce is final tomorrow."

"Great. After that, how would you like to go to Galveston with me?"

"Are you kidding? I can't wait."

"It involves a dog..."

"I love dogs."

Chapter Ten

Richard raced along with traffic on Highway 59 heading into Houston. Music blaring, he bobbed his head in rhythm. No definite plans. No regrets. Lyrics clogged his head drowning out any reason for changing his way of life.

He did notice red and blue lights flashing ahead from the side of the highway. Darting his car across two lanes of oncoming traffic, he zipped into the exit lane. No turn signal, and no encounter with police. Swaying his shoulders, he slowed to enter Little York Road. Scanning the area, he found a car wash, and pulled in with music still blasting.

A bald headed man with a full beard scowled at him, and bolted to the car.

Richard turned off the ignition, and got out.

"What are you doing bringing that noise in here? Man, you want attention?"

"I want my car washed."

"This is my establishment. I don't want any trouble. You come in here, you are on my property. You turn that music down."

Richard nodded, and glanced at the nearby office. It was empty. Looking at the automated car wash building, he spotted only two customers. The owner kept talking, but Richard had lost interest in what the guy had to say.

He paid, and drove his car in the line, minus any music. He thought about the owner while he waited his turn. It wasn't long, and the two cars ahead of him were cleaned, and gone. The automatic switch kicked in and jolted his car along. He sat in the vehicle while it was rinsed, washed, rinsed again, and waxed. While his vehicle chugged out the opposite end of the car wash, he narrowed his eyes at the guy. He watched the owner approach another car.

Richards face wrinkled in contempt.

Rude dude; when you work in the public, the customer is always right.

Richard drove around the block and parked behind a row of tall, evergreen shrubbery. He glared in the direction of the car wash, and withdrew a handful of firecrackers from his glove box. The act of tying each one together on a long string seemed to thrill him. An evil smirk twisted his face as he finished the task. Meandering to the back of the car wash, he still didn't see anyone in the office. Richard slipped to the side door, lit the long string with a match, and pitched it inside the office. Hearing the pop, pop, pop of the fireworks exploding, he ran back to his car, and drove fast to the Eastex Freeway.

Laughing, he imagined the guy in a panic thinking someone was shooting his place to pieces.

Minutes after Richard escaped, a fire truck raced to the car wash. The fire crackers had landed on a couch, and a spark ignited its cloth cover, but

Richard didn't know what his actions caused. He wasn't used to being responsible for his actions, anyway. His mind was already onto something else. He remembered stealing bottles of pain pills.

He reached under the seat with one hand while driving, and felt for a pill bottle. Retrieving it, his car swerved into the next lane side-swiping another vehicle. Never stopping, Richard turned his radio on, and sang along. He opened the bottle, and stuck the tip end of his tongue in it.

The instant the sweet taste of sugar saturated his mouth, he spit it out in a sudden rage. His body trembling, he accelerated, and wildly drove to his drug dealer.

Chapter Eleven

"Thanks for the ride, Pastor Williford. I think I'll walk home when this is over, though, if you don't mind."

"No, ma'am, I understand. We all need our quiet time. I'll go in with you, now, if you want me to."

"That's okay. This is something I need to do by myself."

"Alright, call if you need me."

Lavinia waved by to the Pastor, and entered the courthouse early. Her handbag was checked and cleared by security personnel inside the entrance. She took the elevator to the second floor, and waited in the hall for the double doors of the courtroom to open.

An officer instructed the group to form a single line, and to show proof of identification upon entering the doors. Lavinia, along with many others, displayed her driver's license. The officer pointed to rows of long benches. "Take a seat; wait for your case to be called."

Lavinia glanced at another woman. "Reminds me of church pews; on both sides of the room."

"Must be your first time in court."

"It is, and I like their security measures."

The woman nodded, and they went to the far end of a bench, sat and watched the empty spaces quickly fill. People continued to enter the room until everyone had to squeeze close together making room for others to sit.

The bailiff requested all to be quiet, and silence filled the courtroom.

A side door opened, and Lavinia heard the swish from the long, black robe as the Judge entered.

"All rise. The honorable Judge Ted Poindexter presiding."

Everyone hurried to stand.

The Judge went behind his bench, and sat in the high back chair.

"Be seated." The bailiff announced as he approached the Judge. They conferred while the Judge scanned through a stack of papers.

Lavinia spotted her attorney seated at one of the counsels' tables to the left of the Judge. His presence helped her relax.

"Case of Moore versus Moore."

"I can't believe my case is first." Lavinia looked wide-eyed at the woman next to her, and left the galley. She and her attorney approached the bench.

In a hushed tone the Judge discussed the uncontested divorce between Richard and Lavinia Moore. He acknowledged the absence of Richard Moore in the courtroom, and granted Lavinia the divorce. It was over in seconds. She shook hands with the Judge, and her attorney. The bailiff escorted her to the exit door, and she fought back the urge to run and scream for joy. She emerged into the vacant hallway appearing subdued, but with each step she took, her exhilaration increased.

Stopping at a water fountain on one side of the hallway, she bent to get a drink and in her excitement, choked when she swallowed.

"Are you okay?" An officer advanced toward her, frowning.

Water splattered on her chin, and she tried to smile. "Yes, I'm fine." She wiped the water off with her hand, coughing and sputtering. She finally sounded normal. "I just got my divorce. It's done. I'm free of him!"

The officer's frown disappeared. "Congratulations."

"Thank you."

He hurried to the courtroom, and Lavinia made her way to the elevator. Waiting on it to arrive gave her time to reflect on her new status.

Not married. I'm no longer married to Richard. Oh, thank You, Lord.

The elevator arrived at her floor, and she waited as chattering people got off. The only one left in the elevator, she felt a rush of homesickness, and realized she hardly knew anyone in this town.

No one to share what just happened, a major milestone in my life; my divorce.

Lavinia exited on the ground floor and strolled outside in the fresh morning breeze.

That's silly, I know Kate, and the Pastor, and my attorney, and I'm meeting more people every day.

She walked through the downtown area, and in the distance saw the top of the church steeple. Like seeing an old friend, her mood lightened.

No, I am never alone.

She hummed a favorite old Baptist hymn, then sang the only words she could remember.

Onward, Christian soldiers, marching as we go, with the cross of Jesus, going on before.

She kept singing, and without realizing it, walked faster. Clutching the shoulder strap of her purse with her hand, made it swing back and forth in such a way that her random walk now became a synchronized movement.

Detective Marino noticed her immediately from his office window.

He ran outside and caught up with her.

"Well, that's a happy lady if I've ever seen one." He tried swinging his arms to keep in step with her, and they both laughed.

"I am happy, Detective. I just left
the courthouse. I have been divorced for
almost five minutes." She raised her
shoulders and pranced about.

"Congratulations, and since you're
divorced, now, I'd like you to call me
by my first name; Ben."

She stood still and gave him her
full attention. "Ben, I certainly will."

"Well, thank you, ma'am, and I
hope you don't think I'm being too
forward, but we've already met in the
rain, and now on a bright sunshiny day;
I was wondering if I could take you out
to dinner. That is, unless you have other
plans."

"I'd love to, but I'm going to
Galveston to get a dog."

A mischievous half smile crept over Ben Marino's face. "I thought you just got rid of a dog."

Lavinia burst out laughing.

"I have to go. Ben, I still have to pack, we're leaving before lunch."

"You and who?"

"Kate… Kate Davis."

"Oh, good. Well, at least give me your phone number."

Lavinia pulled a slip of paper from her purse, scribbled her phone number on it, and handed it to him.

"Have a safe trip, lady."

"Thanks, Ben. It was good seeing you."

"You too."

He returned to his office, and she returned to her apartment. Lavinia played their encounter over and over in her mind until she could still picture his mischievous smile even with her eyes wide open.

Chapter Twelve

Kate rang the doorbell at Lavinia's apartment at eleven o'clock—all packed and ready to go. Glad her new friend could make the short trip to Galveston with her, Kate leaned back against the entry wall, at ease, and in no hurry.

Lavinia flung the door open, and stared at Kate.

"Well, hey! Look at you; boots, and blue jeans, and white tank-top, and shades; my, oh my."

Kate laughed. "And aren't you in a great mood, Ms. No Longer Married To A Jerk."

"Yes, I am, and I like your choice of words. Come in, I'm nearly through packing."

Kate strolled inside and removed her sunglasses.

"First time I've seen you wear cowboy boots, Kate. Those I do like. What brand?"

"Thanks. They're Tony Lamas, fit like a glove."

"And look sharp."

"Sounds like we might squeeze in some shopping, Lavinia. We could."

"I'd like that; I haven't been shopping this year."

"This year? Well, you're overdue. And I can't wait to stay overnight in Galveston. The beach will be gorgeous. We'll get the dog tomorrow a few hours before we leave. Gives us plenty of time to sight-see, and go shopping."

"Great. I'll hurry." Lavinia ran into the kitchen, and Kate could hear her opening and closing cabinet doors. She dashed out with a tote full of snacks, grabbing her suitcase and sneakers in the hall.

"Let's do this." She laughed, and they were off.

Kate paused at the entrance gates of Shadowood, punched in her code number, and the security gates slowly opened.

Leaving Houston wasn't easy. Traffic was horrible. For several minutes, a car stayed next to Kate's as if racing side by side, and made a sudden swing propelling the car directly in front of Kate's vehicle.

"Dangerous drivers." Lavinia held onto the front seat.

"Aren't you used to this?"

"Me? No, I am not from the city."

"Lavinia, I thought you lived here in Houston."

"No, Richard does. I'm from the small town of Rosenberg."

"Well, I've lived in Houston for years, and you should have seen me when I first moved here." Kate laughed. "I wouldn't even turn the radio on when I was driving. Couldn't have any distractions. Now I just zip along with them, but I do use my turn signal."

"I've noticed not everyone does."

"So how long have you been in Houston?"

"Four months."

"Mind me asking how you met Richard?"

"No, I don't mind. I just touched on a few things about Richard when I first met you. It's hard to talk about all of it—kind of lengthy, but I have plenty of time now."

"Lavinia, if you'd rather not, I'd understand."

"No, I want to. I met Richard through an online dating site last year. My head was spinning with all the plans he had for us, and first thing you know, I married him. He wanted to live in Rosenberg. Said he quit his job in Houston to be with me, and yes, I supported us on my secretary job in Rosenberg. He could be such a charmer. Anyway, he couldn't keep a job. Found out later he was stealing. He lied constantly. Finally, he wanted us to move to Houston. We did, and I missed my family, my friends, and my job. My whole life changed. We lived with his parents, and they seemed nervous around him. One day he stayed gone for hours, and returned with a car for me, and a lot of money. Paid his parents what he owed them, and made me excited by putting the car in my name. He'd even paid off the car; gave me the bill of sale, and the title."

"Where did the money come from?"

"I couldn't prove it, but I thought it was drugs. He changed after that. Turned mean, and stayed out all night with his friends. I finally had enough, and got a job as temporary office help. Filed for divorce, and paid for it. You know the rest."

"What about his parents?"

"Oh, he had fights with them. They kept accusing him of stealing his mother's jewelry, and his dad's electronic tools. Richard would get angry, but one day he stomped through the house throwing lamps, and turning over furniture. We packed and moved out quick." Lavinia paused glancing at Kate. "I was afraid of what he would do, if I didn't go with him."

Kate nodded.

"After we had our own place for a month, I'd see his friends slip him money when he was outside. I figured his parents were right. He must have been selling what he stole from them."

"Did he get a job?"

"No, he'd stay out until three or four o'clock in the morning. I would cringe when he'd return. He wanted to argue, and I learned not to say anything. The last few weeks I grew more afraid of him. He acted crazy, and he had to be on drugs. You can't imagine how he changed. I felt sorry for his parents."

"Do they know you are divorced?"

"No, but I'd love to drive over to their home, and tell them."

"I wouldn't advise it. Richard could walk in, and it might be more dangerous than the Houston drivers even dare to be."

Lavinia grimaced. "You're right. Richard wouldn't care if he hurt any of us. He has no conscience."

"Thank God your divorce is over, and I'll say one more thing before we change the subject."

"What?"

"He may forget about you, if he's busy with others."

"I hope so."

"Me too. Now, pick out a CD, and let's sing along. Richard is not ruining our fun trip."

Lavinia selected one, and the uplifting tune played as she stretched out, relaxing. Both sang, and sometimes stumbled on the words, improvising the ones they couldn't remember. Laughter filled the car, and memories of Richard were left in Houston.

Galveston was all it promised to be and more. The waves pounding on shore, the ocean breeze, sea gulls—miles and miles of welcomed bliss.

Locating a motel on the beach, Kate paid for a room with two double beds, and they unpacked. Quickly changing into swimsuits, they crammed necessities into a bag, and donned flip-flops. Dashing across the sand, they ran straight to the ocean. Not many tourists were nearby.

Wind in their hair, both removed their shoes and wiggled their toes in the sand at the water's edge.

The fresh saltwater smell overwhelmed them, and they soon sat in the water, embracing the moment. Waves crashed over them, and they leaned their heads back, basking in the sun.

"I'm never leaving." Kate rose and walked until reaching waist deep water, then stretched out, and swam a few yards further.

"Wait." Lavinia caught up and swam beside Kate, each obviously treasuring their ocean time.

Small shore birds scampered across the water's edge going as fast as their tiny legs could carry them. Sea gulls flew overhead diving for food along the beach; screeching as if in play.

A rushing wave collided over Lavinia knocking her under. She bounced back flinging her dripping hair from her face.

"This is heaven." She yelled, and swam into the next oncoming wave.

Kate joined her swimming into the white capped waves. Hollering with pure joy at every wave that engulfed them, neither one realized hours had passed since their arrival.

Both had a look of amazement as the sun began to set.

"Come on, we've got to go."

Lavinia followed Kate back, and they left the ocean as waves rolled onshore dissolving into foam.

Turning to glimpse the picturesque view, they stood in awe. Kate dashed to the tote, and grabbed her cellphone. They quickly took each others picture, finally slipping back into their flip-flops—a leisure day to remember.

The city seemed to come alive as dusk neared. Snatches of conversations carried on the wind as they passed couples and families strolling on the sidewalks.

Hastening to the motel, they were soon ready for the evening.

"So, Kate from New Orleans, what do you recommend for dinner here in Galveston?"

"Kate from New Orleans? Oh, I like that. Well, if it's my choice, I have to say Blackened Redfish. You can't get it as good as they fix it on the Gulf Coast."

"I'll try it. Sounds delectable."

They walked along the sidewalk parallel with the beach and discovered several seafood restaurants overlooking the water. Of course, the sidewalk and the restaurants were a good twenty feet higher than the level of the ocean, but that enhanced the view. Selecting one by its wafting aroma, they were seated in a locally owned restaurant and received excellent food and service. Both took their time eating, savoring every bite.

"What's the name of this fish, again? What did you call it?"

"Blackened Redfish."

"Oh, Kate, it's outstanding. I want this again, sometime."

"We can do it. Galveston isn't that far away."

They couldn't eat all of their salads, and grilled veggies; but both emptied their plate of the fish.

Returning to the motel, they hopped in the car and drove to the ferry crossing.

"This will be the best part of the whole trip. Wait till you ride the ferry at dark with all the flood lights on. The breeze you feel standing on deck puts you in another world. You'll love it."

"I've never been on a ferry boat ride."

"Oh, Lavinia, it's awesome. We'll ride it again in the morning so you can see the ships in the distance. All you can see at night is their lights, but it is amazing. The ships we pass are huge."

"Where are we going?"

"Port Bolivar. I'm glad we got here in time, we'll ride the last one back in an hour."

"You make a good tour guide."

"I was here years ago as a refugee after Hurricane Katrina. We were eventually bused here, and I learned the area."

"I love it."

"So do I."

After the ferry ride back, more pictures were taken. The two drove to the motel and dropped into their beds exhausted, but in a joyful mood.

The next day brought another ferry ride after breakfast. Their shopping left

Galveston minus many souvenirs, and awesome beach paintings. Lunch consisted of scallops and salad with unsweetened tea. They discovered a boot barn around one o'clock and tried on boots for a solid hour. Lavinia found one pair she couldn't do without, and Kate bought a darker pair for winter.

"It's already mid-afternoon, Kate. I love this."

"Me too, but I guess we better go get the dog. I told Ethan we'd have it home around five or six."

"How is he going to take care of it?"

"He planned on hiring a housekeeper today; one that could live there until he was able to fend for himself. He was hoping to get out of the hospital in a few days."

"How sad Ethan's wife died. At least the dog will be some comfort to him."

"Yes. And Ethan said the authorities are conducting an autopsy to determine if her death is a homicide. Poor Becky."

"That's his wife's name?"

Kate nodded. "They were my closest neighbors. And that's why we are going after Rufus. He is adorable, a Yorkshire terrier with the sweetest personality."

They drove to the motel, packed and left. Back on the road, she followed GPS directions to the address Ethan had given her. As they neared it, Kate glanced at Lavinia.

"Can you believe? The police station?"

"That has to be wrong."

Kate parked. "Well, I'm going in. You coming?"

"I'm sure not sitting out here."

They entered, and an officer stared at them from behind the desk.

"Can I help you ladies?"

"Yes sir. I know it sounds strange, but we are here to pick up a dog."

"A dog?"

Kate nodded. "I was told to ask for a Captain Russell."

He reached for his phone and summoned someone to the front desk. They heard the dog barking long before it was spotted in the arms of an officer.

The officer plodded toward the two women while his eyes darted to each face.

"Can you identify yourself?"

"Yes sir. I'm Kate Davis, and this is my friend Lavinia Moore." Kate jerked her driver's license from her billfold and held it out to him. He took it, studied the license for a moment, and returned it to Kate.

"You are the one." He said. "Captain Russell was a code word. We are investigating the death of Becky Meyers, and this was her dog. He's been staying at my house until your arrival. Rufus is an exceptional animal."

He handed the dog to Kate, and Rufus licked her on her nose.

Lavinia tried to stifle a smile but it didn't work.

"I'm Detective Crawford. I'd like to ask you some questions, if you don't mind."

"No, I don't mind."

"So how are you acquainted with Mrs. Meyers?"

"She was my neighbor."

"Did she have any enemies?"

"None that I know of, but I think Steve Anderson might have had ulterior motives being with her and all."

"How is that?"

"He will inherit a lot of money with her dead."

"Did you know Steve Anderson personally?"

"Yes. I didn't trust him. I don't know anyone who did except Becky, but she had just met him. All she knew is that he was her half-brother."

"Thank you, Ms. Davis. I've been told that by a lot of others. I may have to question you further, but Mr. Meyers gave us your phone number. Hopefully, this will be resolved soon. Enjoy your day, ladies, and thanks for transporting the dog back home."

"He doesn't have a kennel or toys?"

"No ma'am." He tipped his hat at Kate and Lavinia, and left.

Rufus wiggled in Kate's arms, and they rushed out to her car. Once seated, he jumped into Lavinia's lap. She fumbled with her seat belt and the dog at the same time. Kate idled the car while retrieving her cellphone, and glanced at her passengers.

"One more picture."

Lavinia positioned the dog's face close to hers.

"Ready?"

"Yes."

Kate focused the camera, and the instant she clicked the button Rufus raised his ears, and Lavinia burst out laughing.

It was a great picture. Kate showed it to Lavinia.

"I want a copy."

"No problem, and I better call Ethan before I put this phone away."

She hit speed dial and waited for him to answer.

"Hello?"

"Ethan, it's me, Kate. You're on my speaker phone. We have Rufus with us and are fixing to leave Galveston. Are you still in the hospital?"

"No, I talked them into letting me come home. They only agreed because I hired a couple to help me. The wife cooks and cleans, and her husband does the lawn and any other maintenance."

"Perfect. I'll drop Lavinia off first, then the dog. We'll be in Houston within an hour."

"Great, and thanks again, Kate."

"You are so welcome." Kate absentmindedly rubbed her right leg, and ended the call. Lavinia noticed the tight pull of fabric over her friend's swollen, lower right leg.

"Out of the car, lady, let's change places. It's my turn to drive." Before Kate could object, Lavinia grabbed Rufus and opened the car door.

"Looks like I better move." Kate slid out from behind the wheel, and stretched back in the passenger's seat.

Lavinia climbed in behind the steering wheel, and deposited Rufus in Kate's lap.

"Now, sit back and relax." She drove onto the street merging with traffic.

"I thought you didn't like driving in Houston?"

"I don't." Lavenia answered solemnly. "But we aren't there yet."

Kate's mouth crinkled into a smile as she turned her face away, and gazed out the window.

"What? What is it?"

"Nothing, Lavenia. I'm just relaxing while I can."

Chapter Thirteen

Dilapidated buildings stood among weed filled vacant lots. Ply board nailed tight over windows were a constant reminder of bygone days. Nothing flourished with the local economy. No business. No jobs. Poverty reeked, block after block in this section of the city.

Richard drove past old store fronts covered in graffiti. A baby wailed from an upstairs apartment as someone peeped through the broken blinds of a grimy window. Shouts of a raging argument penetrated the building into the street below. Richard heard it all. Frustration. Sorrow. Anger.

He drove at a slow pace, taking it all in, and turned his radio volume down. He had never noticed these voices, and kept listening to the neighborhood.

Did he identify with these people? Did he feel anything for them or their situation?

No, Richard only cared about himself. No empathy. His main concern was locating his drug supplier, and the man moved often.

Richard switched radio stations, and heard a preacher speaking. "Ask your Heavenly Father to forgive you of your sins, and really mean it. And stop doing those sins. You don't have to settle for hell because you've been bad. You can have heaven."

Richard paused and frowned before turning to another station. And for the first time, he was aware of others. He was fascinated with the glimpse he encountered.

He turned the corner and drove down another block. An eerie silence greeted him, and he searched for the man. His main man.

Sometimes he saw a shadow dash behind a building, or someone boldly gazing at him from a nearby roof.

Gang members.

He knew their business, and he was a regular customer.

The next block was a replica of the others. No traffic. Nothing. No one walking about. The streets seemed to blend into each other. Almost the same, but Richard couldn't hear anyone. No one shouting. No one crying. No one pleading. He tried to find the preacher on the radio, but lost him. Driving faster, he searched many alleys and streets, and finally spotted his man. Relief flooded his being, and he accelerated.

The man stepped into the vacant street. Richard parked directly in front of him, and placed wads of money into the man's hand. Carefully counting it, he seemed satisfied, and gave Richard several tiny packages containing a white powder. Richard started shaking. The man smiled and waved him off. Richard drove out of the neighborhood and finally parked on the outskirts of a downtown railroad switching yard. Locking his car, he opened one of the packages, and knew he'd pass out soon.

Chapter Fourteen

Driving into Ethan's driveway seemed strange to Kate, after all her own house was directly across the street. Usually she'd walk over to visit Becky, or vice versa. Knowing Becky was gone with her brother could be dealt with, but her being dead and never coming back was mind-boggling.

Ethan sat alone on the porch swing, and even from that distance, Kate could see the pain etched on his face. She realized he was probably a bundle of nerves. Her own nerves were a tangled mess. She'd help him as a Christian, and try to bring some sort of normalcy to this horrific ordeal.

Kate's stepping out of the car with the dog brought Ethan to his feet, and

Rufus, clearly thrilled, barked at Ethan until leaping into his arms. The dog licked Ethan's hands, and arms, and Ethan, teary eyed, hugged him tight.

Kate felt a tug at her heart watching the two reunite.

"He's overjoyed to see you, Ethan. He must have missed you."

"I missed him. I'm glad he's back." Ethan patted the dog, and glanced at Kate. "Thanks for bringing him home."

"We enjoyed it."

Ethan's brow furrowed.

"A friend of mine went with me, Lavinia Moore. I dropped her off a few minutes ago."

"Oh, that's right; you mentioned that before. Well, my thanks to both of you." His face softened, and he nodded toward the porch swing. "Can you stay awhile?"

"Sure."

They ambled to the porch and sat on the two seated, wooden swing with the dog between them.

"How are you holding up? I know this is hard on you."

"It's the not knowing that's the worse part. My imagination doesn't help, either. Kate, her health was fine. How could her body be found near a Houston airport if she simply died? She lived with Steve in Galveston. It doesn't make sense. It has to be a homicide. Steve has to know what happened. And the police call him a person of interest? Who came up with that description anyway?"

"It's just a figure of speech. Like someone trying to be politically correct. Or someone not wanting to offend someone else."

"Why don't they just say they think he murdered her?"

"I guess they are gathering evidence and building a case against him first."

"You're right, but you have to admit Steve is a weird guy."

"I know he is."

Ethan rubbed Rufus behind his ears. "This little guy will be a lot of company for me."

"He is adorable, and I'm sure you were just as glad to get home as he was. How was the hospital stay anyway?"

"Can't complain. Good people working there. Made it tolerable. I certainly don't want to fall down the cellar stairs again."

"Ouch."

"Ouch is right, but I'm walking better, thanks to therapy."

The slow movement of the swing rocking back and forth seemed to calm all of them. Rufus stretched out and went to sleep.

"It is good to be home." Ethan glanced at Kate.

Kate noticed how Ethan seemed to relax. She nodded. "Call me if I can ever help you."

"Thanks, but right now you're doing more help than you know. Just sitting here and talking. I needed that. Hope we can do this again."

"We will. You get some rest, and enjoy your buddy there."

Kate stopped the swing and stood still a moment.

"Ethan, I have new neighbors next door, and I want to invite them to church, along with my new friend, Lavinia. Think you'd feel up to going to church with us sometime?"

"Yes ma'am, I do."

"Good. We'll talk later. By."

"By."

Kate went to her car, backed out of his driveway, drove a few feet to cross the street and pulled straight into her own driveway. She exited her car, and waved at Ethan. He gave her an enthusiastic wave back and went inside his house with Rufus.

Her mood had lightened, and she no longer struggled with the idea of visiting Ethan with Becky gone. No one could help Becky now.

Kate glanced across the street, again.

Hmm, it didn't seem so strange driving in his driveway after all.

Chapter Fifteen

Pastor Williford dropped Lavinia off for her job interview at the school, and waited in his car. Children behind locked gates shouted as others ran by enjoying the playground. Chains from the occupied swing sets creaked loudly, and many children shouted from the monkey bars. Lavinia smiled as she approached the main entrance to the elementary school building.

A security guard checked her identification and escorted her inside.

Surveillance cameras recorded every movement. A sign four feet tall and four feet wide boldly stated this was not a gun-free zone. It warned that students were protected by armed guards and armed staff. Unauthorized admittance was not allowed.

Several schools in Texas had adopted the same security measures, and they were overwhelmingly approved and supported by the community.

A shrill bell rang, and the playground emptied as students entered the building. Pastor Williford opened his Bible, and read, intermittently stopping to scan the area.

A man in his mid twenties had been strolling by when he paused and veered toward the parking lot. He carried a plastic grocery bag, and Pastor Williford locked his car.

Once the younger man entered the parking lot, he began pacing the back end of it near a line of trees. Intrigued, the Pastor focused on the man.

Was he waiting for someone? Did he really have groceries in the bag?

Mindful of possibilities, the Pastor remembered the security training their church had received, and viewed situations in a different manner than he would have a few years ago.

A school security vehicle with two officers drove into the parking lot. The man stood still the instant he saw it. The driver drove the vehicle straight at the man, and he bolted. The other officer rushed from the vehicle chasing the man on foot. He swung his bag at the officer, hitting his upper arm, and the second security officer rushed from the car. Pastor Williford left his car, and remembering to use his cane, he hurried to the men. He arrived as one officer hand-cuffed the man, and called the police.

"I was coming to help. What did he have in the bag?"

Moaning, the man in handcuffs rolled onto his stomach, and lay on the parking lot.

"A brick. Stay back sir."

Pastor Williford did what the officer requested, and heard a siren drawing near.

"I'm Pastor Williford. I'll wait by my car."

"Thanks for trying to assist. I'll talk to you in a minute."

"I'm hot." The man screamed, and stood, trying in vain to remove his clothes with the handcuffs on. He jerked at his pants and shirt until he fell. The officer grabbed him before his head hit the ground. The second officer called for EMS assistance. Both officers held the man down as he slammed his fists at them.

The ambulance arrived, and it took three men to place him on the gurney. He did manage to rip his shirt. Finally strapped tight, they wheeled him inside the ambulance, and took his vital signs.

Pastor Williford leaned against his car and gazed in amazement.

One of the security officers approached the Pastor, and shook hands with him.

"Ever hear of Wet?"

"No sir, I haven't."

"It's the street name of an illegal drug that makes the users feel on fire. I've seen them strip their clothes off in an intersection full of traffic, and fight with super human strength when arrested. It takes several men to restrain someone on Wet. Days later they don't remember it even happened."

"And he was right here on the school parking lot."

"Yes sir, they can't think or reason on drugs."

"So what happens to him now?"

"His first stop is to the hospital."

They watched as the police officer left following the ambulance.

"It's all over, Pastor. You can go on now."

"Oh, I'm waiting on a friend of mine. She's getting interviewed for a job at the school."

"Let's hope this doesn't scare her away."

"Well, it's not like this happens every day, officer."

"Unfortunately, it does. We just don't know where."

Pastor Williford nodded at him, and the security officer left with his partner. Opening his car door, he sank into the front seat, and locked the car. Birds chirped, and a breeze rustled through the nearby trees.

Like a normal day, no clue a drug addict was just arrested here.

He glanced at his watch. An hour had passed since Lavinia entered the school.

Minutes later, he watched as someone walked her to the entrance gates, and let her out. The gates were locked, and Lavinia proceeded down the sidewalk towards him.

She glanced at her cell phone, and stopped to text a message. Hurrying to the Pastor's car, she couldn't contain her excitement as she got in the front seat. Face all aglow, she put on her seat belt fast, and turned to look at him.

"Guess what? That was Ben, I mean Detective Marino. My car needed repair, but he said it was regular maintenance. Nothing was sabotaged. They can't prove Richard did anything to it."

"You get your car back?"

"Yes, isn't that great? And I can finally get my belongings out of the car! Oh, and I'll know next week if I get the job, or not."

"Well, I'm happy for you. Want me to drive you over to the police station to get your car?"

"Thanks, but no, Detective Marino is bringing it to me."

"Sounds like a plan."

"It is." Lavinia beamed.

Chapter Sixteen

"Mr. Meyers, you have company."

Ethan looked past his housekeeper at the uniformed police officer in the doorway.

"Make yourself comfortable." He stood and gestured to lounge chairs on the patio. The officer hung his head, and the housekeeper hurried back inside the house.

Ethan's cordial smile disappeared as he studied the officer.

"It's about Becky. Isn't it?"

"I'm sorry, sir."

"Was she murdered?"

"Yes sir."

Ethan edged toward the overgrown pot of pencil cactus and

fingered a long, green stem. Staring across the lawn he seemed mesmerized by something off in the distance. The officer stepped closer to him, and Ethan turned making eye contact.

"I once told her she was like this plant. It takes off in one direction, and then grows another maze of branches at another angle, spontaneous like her. No plan for the future, just jump and do things with no thought of the consequences."

Both men meandered to the lounge chairs and eased into them.

"It was Steve, wasn't it? He did it, didn't he?"

The officer nodded. "We had to wait for DNA evidence, and finally got the report back this morning. I wanted to tell you in person before you heard it on the news."

"I didn't know it was on television." Ethan gazed out at the lawn again.

"I worked another case this one ties into. I requested to be the one to tell you."

"Tell me."

"Do you remember when Joe Ingram was killed here?"

"Of course I do. It happened right across the street. Wade Banning was indicted. He's in jail waiting for his trial."

"Well, Mr. Banning was also involved in a lot of burglaries in the neighborhood. He even robbed your pocket watch from your house and claimed Steve Anderson paid him to do it. Said Steve wanted to discredit you as a Peeping Tom, and dropped your watch in Kate Davis' shrubbery. It would have been Steve's word against Wade's until we found the murder weapon."

"The murder weapon?"

"Wade Banning stole it long before he was arrested. Steve paid him for it."

"Well, Steve sure kept it a long time."

"We never knew the gun existed until recently."

"The gun? But I thought at first they weren't sure if it was a homicide. Wouldn't that mean no gunshot wounds?"

"There were no gunshot wounds."
Ethan frowned.

"There is no other way to say this, but he shot her with a veterinarian's high powered tranquilizer gun. The poisoned darts would have knocked an elephant to the ground leaving it lifeless in minutes."

Ethan gulped back a sob and punched his fist into the metal serving tray. It caved in and all four legs collapsed. Glaring at the officer he shouted, "She couldn't stand needles, and now I find out she died by poisoned darts?"

"Mr. Meyers, she died instantly. She was shot in the neck."

Chapter Seventeen

Kate kicked the soccer ball to the Hernandez kids. Running to it, they squealed with joy and kicked it back to her.

She kicked hard with her left foot, and the ball shot into their front lawn. Maria ran out of their garage holding a dish cloth in her hand.

"What's this commotion?"

Kate's eyes seemed to sparkle, and she rushed toward her neighbor. "I bought them a soccer ball. I hope you don't mind."

"Oh, you spoil them. They will not forget it. Thank you."

She glanced at her children. "Stay in the back yard with the ball, and thank the lady."

"Thank you." They spoke in unison, and dashed off with the ball toward the fenced back yard.

"How's the unpacking going?"

Maria raised her hands to the sky. "Thank the Lord, I am done." She spoke in an emotion filled voice. "And thank you for your casserole. It was delicious, and so needed that tiring day."

She marched straight to Kate and hugged her.

Speechless, Kate smiled at her new neighbor enjoying the sudden gesture of friendship.

They stepped back and both seemed aware of a special bonding.

"Maria, I would like for you and your family to join me at my church this Sunday. I know you don't know anyone there, but this is God's house, and we worship together."

"I will feel comfortable. If you are there, we will be there. Tell me where and what time."

"Christ Community Church. Starts at 10:45 Sunday morning."

"We will meet you there."

Kate nodded, felt like jumping up and down, and returned to her home.

Throwing a load of dirty clothes in the washing machine, she went about her weekly routine of cleaning. Dismissing the sound of something shrill, she vacuumed the living room carpet deciding it was the phone, and she wasn't stopping her day for a telemarketer.

The instant she finished and unplugged the vacuum cleaner, she recognized it was the ring of the doorbell; shrill and constant.

Alarmed, she raced to the front door, and flung it open.

Ethan stood with a pale complexion, and a pained stare.

Kate grabbed him by his arms.

"Talk to me, Ethan. What is it?"

"It's Becky, she's all over the news."

Kate pulled him inside her home.

"I'm so sorry."

He nodded. "Turn on the television."

"Are you sure?"

"Turn it on."

She took him into the living room veering him to her recliner. He eased into it while she clicked the remote, and sat on the couch.

The television blasted on in high volume. The words "Breaking News" raced across the screen to the pulsating loud music jangling nerves by the sound alone, much less the forthcoming message.

Kate and Ethan, attentive and quiet, listened as the announcer gave the update on the case. A picture of Steve Anderson's mug shot was displayed. He had a rowdy appearance. The announcer kept talking, kept giving details neither Kate nor Ethan wanted to hear, yet were afraid to miss.

And then it was over. Television resumed to regular programming.

Kate approached Ethan who lay in the recliner with his eyes closed.

"Ethan, we'll get through this. With God's help we'll make it. And I want you to go to church with me next Sunday. We need God's Word for strength."

Ethan nodded and squeezed her hand.

Chapter Eighteen

Upon seeing Kate and Ethan enter
the church; Pastor Williford approached
the entrance. Embracing Ethan in a bear
hug, the two men held onto each other.

"I'm so sorry, Ethan."

Ethan choked out the words,
"Thank you."

Others surrounded him with hugs
offering their condolences. Impressed
by their concern, Ethan stepped back
from the group.

"I haven't felt this much love in a
long time. Everyone needs a church
family like I have." A heartfelt smile
filled his face.

Kate noticed Lavinia approach and
grabbed Ethan's arm.

"I want you to meet a new friend of mine. Ethan, this is Lavinia Moore." She turned to Lavinia. "And Lavinia, this is my neighbor, Ethan Meyers."

"Sorry to meet you under these circumstances, Mr. Meyers, and I'm so sorry for your loss."

"Thanks you, and it's Ethan, not Mr. Meyers. Lavinia, I can't think of a better place I'd rather be today. It's good to meet you."

A young girl ran to him and tugged at his pants leg. "Hi, Mr. Ethan."

He glanced down at Aleesha and placed his hands on his hips, smiling warmly.

"Well, if it isn't the girl who sings like an angel. I hope you're singing something for us this morning."

"I sure am. I have to go get ready." She darted off to the other end of the church. Her father, Daniel Star, and stepmother T9C, made their way to Ethan.

Ethan received more condolences as Lavinia pulled Kate aside.

"Looks like a great idea bringing him to church today."

"I agree. He's handling this well."

The Hernandez family arrived as soft music began playing. Kate made fast introductions, and they all hastened to crowd into a pew.

Pastor Williford made his way to the pulpit and welcomed everyone, especially the visitors. Aleesha Star sang solo. Her young voice filled the sanctuary with 'It Is Well With My Soul.' Everyone applauded when she finished, and the little, seven year old girl with long, straight, brown hair curtseyed; and quickly ran to the choir loft.

Pastor Williford smiled as she made her exit. "She is such a blessing."

He said the prayer followed by singing from the congregation, and two songs by the choir.

Pastor Williford began his sermon with a smile on his wrinkled face. You could see every sermon this man had ever preached within every wrinkle in his skin. "I want you to think about something today. Have you tried to talk to someone about God? Have you been brushed off? 'Oh, I believe in God', they say. Really? Are you saying you believe there *is* a God, or are you saying

you *know* God?" He paused and
scanned the congregation.

"If you ask them that question,
they will quit the conversation fast, and
walk away. I have learned in talking to
someone to ask what their spiritual
preferences are. I tell them what mine
are and invite them to visit our church
for worship."

" I would love for everyone to end
up in Heaven. But it's a matter of
choice; Heaven or Hell. So, the point
I'm making is to try and offer everyone
the opportunity while the opportunity is
still here." He paused again and raised
his eyebrows.

"If someone tells you they know
God, ask them this; are you stating a
fact? Like you'd state a baseball bat is
used to hit a baseball? In the same

sense, are you stating you know there is a God? Or can you describe it further by saying; I know God, He is a loving God, God the Father, Son, and Holy Ghost. I have received Him, I am committed to Him, I ask for His guidance, and His will in my life. I ask for forgiveness of my sins, and earnestly try not to *repeat* those sins. Folks, there is a big difference in *knowing* God, and knowing there *is* a God."

He read scripture from Proverbs 6: 16-19, and continued his sermon.

"A world that does not worship God is a dangerous place. It's hostile, has conflict. Be not conformed to this world. Do the will of God. For the wages of sin is death."

"Turn now to Romans 10:9-17." He read the scripture, and closed his

Bible. "I leave you with hope, and how to receive the Lord Jesus. If anyone wants to make a decision to proclaim Jesus as your Savior, or dedicate your life to Christ, or join the church; I'll be waiting at the pulpit for you while we sing."

The congregation sang 'Just As I Am' and on this occasion no one came forward. The service ended with another prayer.

Music played as the crowd exited the church one pew at a time.

Ethan and Sal struck up a conversation, and Maria joined Kate and Lavinia as another woman rushed to Ethan.

"Mr. Meyers, you may not remember me. Becky was in my Sunday school class. I'm Carolanne Marshall. I heard the news this morning. So tragic. My heart goes out to you, and you are in my prayers."

"Thank you, ma'am. It was a shock to everyone."

Sal grabbed Ethan by his arm and walked him toward the parking lot. He continued talking as if they weren't interrupted.

Rosa and Carlos walked near their mother both chattering about the girl who sang solo.

"I can't believe it." Kate held her hand to her chest. "I thought Carlos couldn't speak English. He didn't when I first met him."

"Oh, that's my mother's fault. She doesn't speak English, and she's been visiting us. She is back home in Monterrey, Mexico now. But because of her, Carlos is well-versed in both languages."

"When he's older, he'll be first in line for a job. Being bilingual is a bonus."

"That's my Carlos, a big talker in any language." Maria had a quick playful grin until she noticed a gray haired woman approach Lavinia.

The woman tapped on the back of Lavinia's shoulder. Lavinia turned giving the woman an incredible stare, and blurted, "Aren't you my attorney's receptionist?"

She looked straight at Lavinia. "Yes, I'm Julie Nugent. I hope you have a minute. I'd like to talk to you."

"Go ahead."

"I owe you an explanation. That day I was eavesdropping at the door, well, I didn't know you. I am sorry to say I made a wrong assumption about you."

Lavinia frowned. "I don't understand."

"Well, I'm embarrassed now, please forgive me. I thought you were a young flirt, because so many in your age group are these days. Young twenties, I mean. Anyway, I was looking out for my boss. He has such a thoughtful wife, and they have an awesome marriage. I was going to step inside his office if I heard you say anything suggestive."

"Mrs. Nugent, thank you for your honesty. Of course I forgive you. I think we all have issues with trying not to assume things. Sometimes we don't wait to get the facts. And I admire you for explaining, but I hope I don't seem like a flirt to others."

Julie Nugent leaned toward the younger woman and hugged her.

"No, you don't seem like that at all, now. I was judging what I wanted to see then, and shouldn't have been judging at all."

"We all make mistakes. Don't give it another thought."

With a smile that faded quickly, the older lady left swerving through the crowd.

"Well, that took a lot of gumption. Not many would admit what she told you."

Lavinia looked at Kate. "You're right."

"You know what that means don't you?"

"No, what?"

"We're going to take her a casserole."

Sal and Ethan paused in their conversation, and one of them groaned. "Did someone mention casserole?"

Maria looked at the men. "It was only a mention. Why is anyone hungry?"

Lavinia raised her head displaying a slow smile. "I am."

"Fried chicken kind of day? That's my favorite kind of day." Kate edged toward Ethan. "What do you think?"

Ethan and Sal exchanged a glance, and both nodded.

Chapter Nineteen

Becky Meyers funeral was finally held. The Houston Chronicle photographed Steve Anderson, her half-brother, as police officers escorted him into the Harris County jail. He smirked at the camera and wouldn't comment about her death. The case no longer made breaking news. A few days earlier, a weather forecaster informed local residents of a hurricane forming in the Gulf Coast and gaining strength.

Most didn't pay attention. It was hurricane season, but too early to predict its path.

Today's morning news mentioned the hurricane, again. Kate raised her head when its name was announced.

"Hurricane Harvey." She repeated out loud.

Kate's phone rang, and she glanced at the caller ID; Lavinia Moore.

"Hey girl."

"Kate? I'm going to visit Richard's parents."

"That's dangerous. Don't do it." Kate heard shallow breathing on the phone. "Lavinia? Did you hear me?"

"I'm leaving now."

Kate felt her stomach convulse.

"He's there isn't he?"

"Yes. I'll see you tomorrow."

The phone went dead, and Kate trembled dialing 9-1-1.

"Harris County, what's your emergency?"

"A friend of mine is being kidnapped. I need to talk to Detective Marino immediately."

"What is your name, ma'am?"

"I'm Kate Davis. Please, just get him on the phone. He knows my friend, she is Lavinia Moore."

"One moment."

Kate stared at the phone and prayed silently.

Minutes later Detective Marino answered.

"Ms. Davis? What's going on?"

"Lavinia called. She sounded strained. Said she was going to Richard's parent's house. I know she'd never do that. I asked her if Richard was there, and she said yes, she'd see me tomorrow, and then the call ended."

"I'll get unmarked cars at her apartment now. Stay where you are, and lock your doors."

He hung up, and she ran through the house checking if outside doors were still locked. They were. She quick made another call.

"Pastor Williford?"

"Kate? You don't sound right."

"I'm not." Her voice cracked. "It's Lavinia. I think her ex-husband kidnapped her. I called the police, and they are coming in unmarked cars. I want you to go and lock all of your doors right now. Take the phone with you, but don't talk in case Richard is outside. Be quiet."

"I will be extra quiet."

She heard the faint sound of his footsteps, and waited.

He returned and spoke in a low voice. "My doors are all locked, and I saw Lavinia's car in her driveway. Didn't see anyone outside her apartment, though."

"The police will be arriving any minute."

"Call that detective friend of hers."

"I did."

"What's his name?"

"Ben Marino."

"Let's get off the phone, I need to listen."

"Okay."

She ended the call, and sat in the recliner rubbing her arms. Grabbing the remote, she turned the television off. Thoughts of Lavinia grew into worse case scenarios flashing through her mind. Refusing to be pessimistic, Kate prayed again. She rose from the recliner and meandered toward the living room window noticing how gray it was outside. Steady rain fell as she paced and waited.

She jerked when her phone abruptly rang. Snatching it with a shaky hand, she didn't bother looking at the caller ID.

"Hello?"

"Kate? This is Detective Marino. We've searched the apartment. She's gone, but we'll find her. His parents are being questioned now. We have the make and model of Richards car, and we already have a warrant out for his arrest. They can't disappear."

"No, they can't."

"If you hear from either of them, let us know."

"I will, and I just realized I don't know what Richard looks like."

"Give me your e-mail address, and I'll send a picture of him."

Kate gave him the information, thanked him for calling, and hurried to call Ethan. He answered on the second ring.

"Good morning, Kate."

"Ethan, can you come over?"

"I'm almost there."

He knocked on her front door within seconds, and she marveled to herself how nice it was he lived across the street.

She let him inside, and he immediately frowned upon seeing her.

"What's wrong?"

"It's a long story. Lavinia's gone."

"Let's get some coffee. Have you had breakfast?"

"No, I can't eat."

"You have to eat something. Wait here, I'll get my car."

He returned with his car and held an umbrella over Kate as he walked her to the passenger's car door. Once settled in the car, he turned to her with concern etched on his face.

"Now what's this about Lavinia being gone?"

Kate filled him in on the details. He drove to the nearest IHOP restaurant, and they dashed inside. Rain continued as they ordered and sipped hot coffee.

"How did Richard find her?"

"I don't know. I told the Detective while ago that I don't even know what Richard looks like. He's sending me a picture of him by e-mail."

"Have you checked it lately?"

"No, but I will."

She clutched her phone and thumbed through several e-mails when she spotted it.

"Here it is. She touched the attachment and Richard's face appeared.

They both bent over the phone and viewed the image.

"He'd scare a hungry dog off a meat wagon."

Kate laughed.

They ate their breakfast and had their coffee refilled.

Kate enjoyed Ethan's presence. She took another sip of coffee and realized her hand was no longer shaking. They left, and drove back to Shadowood. At the entrance, a car was going past the open security gate, and Ethan followed, finally parking at Kate's house.

Once inside, Kate's eyes softened; filled with an inner glow. "It's better when someone waits with you. Thanks for coming Ethan, and thanks for breakfast."

"Oh, I'm still waiting. I'm not going anywhere."

A knock on the front door startled both of them, and Kate squinted through the peephole.

"It's Detective Marino."

Kate opened the door, and ushered him in from the pouring rain.

After introducing the men to each other, Detective Marino grimaced, and looked at Kate.

"Lavinia is safe. She's in a private hospital."

"What? A hospital?" Kate paled, and every fiber of her body tensed with fear.

Ethan placed his hand on Kate's shoulder, and it seemed to calm her.

The detective continued.

"Richard fought her while he was driving, and she escaped when he stopped at a red light. She has some broken teeth, but her jaw isn't broken. We're keeping her there for an oral surgeon to do the repairs tomorrow."

"Thank God you found her as soon as you did. And Richard Moore? What about him?"

"Richard Moore is on his way to jail."

Chapter Twenty

"Did you hurt her?" Mr. Moore spoke in a solemn manner exiting the police station.

"Oh, so you believe them?"

"I posted your bail, son. They didn't arrest you without a good reason."

Richard stopped walking down the courthouse steps and whirled around; a hateful smirk on his face. "Don't start nothing."

The complete opposite of Richard; Mr. Moore stood still in his Ivy League button down shirt, and wrinkle- free dress pants. With his thinning white hair neatly combed, he stopped and stared at his son. Richard wore his usual rumpled shirt, and dirty jeans.

"I'm out of here, old man."
Richard pivoted, and sprinted down the remainder of the steps. Strolling away, he had a cocky walk, and never looked back at his father.

"No, I am." Mr. Moore spoke to himself and left the courthouse with caution. No longer seeing Richard eased his mind, but the threat stayed with him each step he took.

Returning home, he went directly to the kitchen and joined his wife. She poured them both a cup of coffee, and they sat in the breakfast nook.

"Where is he?"

"With his friends, I guess."

"How is Lavinia? I love her like a daughter."

"We both do." He lowered his head, rubbed the back of his neck, then glanced at his wife. "I heard she'll be fine after some dental work."

Mrs. Moore cringed.

"And I heard they are divorced. I'm sure she'll get a restraining order against him."

"He's not our old Richard anymore."

"No, he's not, and that's why I decided something on the way home." He placed his cup in his saucer and gave his wife his full attention. "We're moving."

She sat up straight, and alert.

"I always hoped when we retired we could find a quiet place in the country. Maybe we could start looking around and move in a few months."

"Not in a few months. I don't trust Richard. I'm calling a moving company today. They can have us packed and loaded in a few days. And I'll get a Realtor on the phone. Richard just got bailed out by our savings for the last time."

Chapter Twenty-One

Lavinia opened her eyes and thought she saw Ben Marino sitting in a chair. Groggy, she scanned the room and realized she was in a hospital bed. Her mouth throbbed. She flinched as her hand brushed across her bruised and swollen face.

"Hey, ladybug. Glad you're awake." Ben's eyes brightened, and he smiled.

"You have a sweet smile, Ben."

"Somewhere in there, you do too. I hope to see it again, soon."

Lavinia sat up and blinked, reaching to touch the side of her face, again.

"Doc got you fixed up. You need time to heal now."

His words seemed to jog her memory. A flash of temper narrowed her eyes.

"Richard? Where is he?"

Ben pressed his lips together in a tight line, and frowned. "Out on bond, but don't worry. I'm taking you to a safe place. He won't find you."

"A safe place?"

"Well, I couldn't work and worry about you at the same time."

"Oh Ben, thank you."

"My brother and his wife live in Jacksonville in East Texas. I've already talked to them. Soon as we get a restraining order against Richard, I'm driving you there. We'll get your belongings from the apartment, and you'll be spending the night with them tonight."

"What about my car?"

"I think you should sell it at a car lot before we leave."

She pressed the hospital call button.

"Yes?" An alert voice answered from the nurses' station.

"I'm ready to get out of here." She glanced at Ben, and tried to smile.

Chapter Twenty-Two

Kate stared at the picture on the television screen. Taken from space, she knew the horrific massiveness of Hurricane Harvey would forever be embedded in her mind. The announcer gave its increase in speed and size, and Kate stood in front of the television, and cried.

She cried for the coming destruction, for families that would be torn apart, for lives lost and others changed permanently, loss of homes, loss of jobs, and loss of a way of life she knew many could never return to or rebuild.

She rushed outside through the heavy rain and ran to the home of her next door neighbors, Sal and Maria

Hernandez. Pounding on their front door, she burst inside the instant the door opened.

"Pack right away, and come with me. We have to leave. This hurricane is too dangerous."

Maria gave a frightened glance at her husband, and he approached Kate.

"Where will you go?"

"North East Texas, I'm going to Ethan's and have him come also. And I'll call Lavinia, and Pastor Williford."

"I'll call Ethan to come over." Sal phoned his friend, and Ethan arrived in minutes.

Kate hurried to his side, and looked at Maria.

"Maria, turn on your television. They're showing pictures of the hurricane taken from space. You can look at its size and see why we have to leave."

Maria grabbed the remote and clicked it on.

The awesome mass of the hurricane was displayed from different angles.

Kate and Ethan, wet and shivering, huddled with their friends, and watched in silence.

Finally, Ethan spoke. "I'll drive. My Suburban will seat all of us, and has more cargo space. Let's start packing, and leave right away."

"I'm not going." Sal spoke with a blank expression on his face.

Maria clutched his arm, frowning. "We go together."

"No, I will stay to watch the neighborhood. I have to protect our homes."

"But we are a family."

"You, Carlos, and Rosa will be fine with Ethan and Kate. Maria, I have to stay and keep looters out. This is our home."

Ethan and Sal exchanged a knowing glance, and Ethan addressed Maria.

"We might not be gone but a few days, but we must go quickly."

Sal handed Kate his phone. "Call the pastor. He is too old to remain here alone."

Kate grabbed the phone, punched his number in, and he answered on the first ring.

"Pastor Williford here."

"It's me Kate. I'm putting you on speaker phone. I'm with Ethan, and the Hernandez family. We want you to ride with us and leave before the hurricane makes landfall."

"I don't think it's going to be that bad. The mayor hasn't said anything about evacuating."

"Was he in Hurricane Katrina?"

"I don't know."

"Well, I was, and I'm not going through that again. Sitting in your attic with no help coming, no food, no drinking water, no cell phone service; and no way out except on the roof? And the water keeps rising? No."

"Where are you going?"

"Northeast Texas. One of the Texas shelters open during Hurricane Katrina was in a town called Marshall at the Civic Center; maybe they will open it again. I did hear a reporter say that all State Parks would shelter evacuees. Caddo Lake State Park is in Karnack, near Marshall and has cabins."

"I think you all should go, but I'm staying here."

"No, Pastor, we want you to come with us."

"I appreciate your concern, but I'm not going. We might have looters, and I'm not letting that happen here."

Sal spoke immediately. "Pastor, this is Sal Hernandez. I'm staying here too for the same reason. We'll keep in touch. Kate wants to call Lavinia and see if they can pick her up at the hospital. I'm sure she'll want to go with them."

"That detective called me an hour ago. He said he's moving Lavinia to East Texas. Her ex-husband, Richard Moore got out of jail. He knocked out some of her teeth, but she is recovering from surgery."

"She'll be safer away from here." Sal and the Pastor exchanged phone numbers and ended the call.

Ethan scanned the group. "Pack enough clothes for a week, take photo albums, important papers, any medicines, snacks, canned food, bottled water, blankets, pillows, books, toys for the kids, flashlights, anything else you can think of. We'll meet back here in an hour, and leave just before lunch. I want us to pray for safe travels, and for all of our protection."

Grim faces nodded, and they each hurried in different directions.

Ethan returned home, warning his housekeeper and her husband of the approaching danger. Upon hearing Ethan's plans, they decided to leave immediately for West Texas to visit family.

Chapter Twenty-Three

Low lying areas around Houston filled with the usual flooding. Packed and buckled in, the small group of neighbors stared out the car windows as Ethan drove them through the pouring rain.

They weren't alone. Highways were full with like-minded residents. Ethan drove past long lines that had formed at gas stations. He always tried to kept a full tank of gas in his vehicle or at least leave it three quarters full. Today he was grateful for the full tank. He glanced at Kate sitting in the passenger seat next to him holding his dog, Rufus. They didn't know how grateful he was to have them in his life.

Kate certainly had no idea how important she had become to him.

And he was glad to have his neighbors in the back seat; Maria and her children were nervous without Sal. None of them had stayed at the Caddo Lake State Park before, but it had good reviews, and at least they had a destination that was expecting them. Kate had called and made the arrangements. He stole another glance at her. He noticed how peaceful she seemed, and felt an overwhelming burst of emotion well up inside of him.

I've fallen in love with her, and she doesn't know.

Maria glanced at the silent couple in the front seat, and gripped her cellphone. It had a full charge, and she started scrolling for weather alerts. A map of Texas displaying recent rainfall measurements caught her attention.

"Hey!" Her voice rose in alarm. "It's flooding along the coast and in many towns inland."

Ethan looked at Maria in his rear view mirror. "More will be leaving. I hope they get out in time."

"So do I."

Kate twisted to one side, frowning at Maria. "The traffic will get worse. We should be at the State Park in Karnack by four o'clock this afternoon." Kate motioned to the two children yawning. "Try to take a nap while you can."

Maria adjusted her small pillow and pulled the children close to her. They lay sprawled across the seat, one on each side of her. She closed her eyes, and with the hum of the automobile; the three were soon sleeping.

Kate whispered to Ethan. "Let me take a turn at driving. You haven't been out of the hospital long. You must be tired."

"No, I'm fine, that's why they let me out." He whispered back.

She narrowed her eyes at him, and half smiled. "Is this going to be a problem?"

"No, I'm too happy with you to have a problem." He raised his eyebrows at her and winked.

"Ethan, watch the road. And what are you doing winking at me?" She gave him a dazed look and playfully swatted him on his arm.

"Ma'am, remind me to finish this conversation later."

"I will. Would you like a snack or a bottle of water?"

"Water would be great."

Kate snatched a bottle from the cooler, and handed it to him.

"Thanks. Why don't you find your pillow and get comfortable?"

"I will."

Kate searched through an over-sized tote bag sitting at her feet and located a small pillow. Propping her head with it against the side of the seat, she smiled at Ethan, and fell asleep.

The four of them awoke when the car stopped.

Kate saw the tall pine trees and knew where they were. Ethan could be seen talking to a Park Ranger at the Ranger's Station.

"We're here. We made it to Caddo Lake State Park." Kate opened her car door, got out and stretched.

Maria and her children left the vehicle while they all talked at the same time. Chattering continued as the children spotted a map showing a play area with swings and picnic tables.

Ethan walked back to the car, and appeared weary.

"They don't take pets."

Kate winced. "I forgot to ask."

"It's okay. He recommended several places that board pets in Marshall. Why don't all of you use the restroom while we're here, and I'll call one of them before they close. I'm sure they'll wait on us if we hurry."

"We'll hurry."

They arrived with Rufus in fifteen minutes. Arrangements were made, food and toys were left with the dog, and they returned to the State Park before dark.

The cabins were wonderful. Ethan had his own one bedroom cabin, and Maria, Kate and the children shared a two bedroom cabin. Complete with microwave, refrigerator, stove, A.C., beds, and outdoor grill; the cabins were located near the playground. Carlos and Rosa played while the car was unpacked. The Park Ranger treated them to a wiener roast around a camp fire later at dusk. At first, crackles from the fire as the wood burned and sap popped seemed to echo through the woods. Later, crickets and tree frogs brought their own blend to the outdoor melody.

Ethan blessed the food and gave thanks for a safe trip.

As the stars came out in the unclouded sky, a hoot owl startled Carlos with its loud and repeated cry.

"Shh, it's in the tree behind me. Listen." Carlos bent over and crept towards the nearest pine and oak trees.

"Carlos, come back. You can't see what's there." Maria stood with her hands on her hips. One look at his mother, and he rushed wide-eyed back to the campsite.

The Park Ranger passed out long, metal rods, and the sweet scent of roasted marsh-mellows lingered in the night air. The quick flame on the tip of a marsh-mellow on each rod had the group eating fast and wanting more. Anxiety from the Hurricane seemed to lessen as the group of neighbors relaxed around the campfire. Later, Carlos and Rosa put the campfire out with gallon jugs of water before the Ranger left. They thanked him and immediately begged to go swing.

"Such energy! Okay, let's go swing." Maria laughed at her children, and they raced to the well-lit playground.

Ethan approached Kate and reached for her hand. "Care for a walk along the road? I want to stay by the street lights."

"Sure."

They walked surrounded by woods enjoying the mild breeze coming from the coast.

"About that conversation we didn't finish earlier." He paused, and stopped walking.

Kate raised her face to him and appeared confused.

"I'm in love with you."

Her face softened, and she touched his cheek with her hand. "I feel honored, but I'm not the right one for you."

"I know who's right for me, lady."

"You don't understand. I have disabilities; I don't want to burden you with them. You need someone who can join you in whatever you do."

"And I know you can, we both have limits, Kate. I love you, and I know you love me. I've seen it in your eyes."

"You're right, but I want you to think about something. You've been married before, and I haven't. I don't want to be compared to Becky. I'm not her. I don't want to condone her, because I did like her, and she'll always be a part of your life. You were used to her."

"I think I know what you are trying to say."

"Wait, let me finish." Kate frowned, and bit the inside of her lip. "I have to say this, and I won't mention it again. I didn't like how she treated you. I never saw her do anything with you, or for you, or even to help you. Ethan, please don't have low expectations of all women because of her. If I'm to be your new wife, I want you to see me for who I am. Don't be afraid that I'd ever change and end up like her. Give me a chance to be me. I'd be miserable in her shadow."

"Kate, she's part of my past, yes, that's true. But the past is just that, the past. No shadows. I want us together in the future. Marry me, say yes."

He bent down and kissed her before she could speak another word.

Trembling, she returned his kiss.

"That's a yes, isn't it?"

"Yes, yes it is."

They looked at each other beaming. Ethan squeezed her hand, and they strolled back to the others.

Chapter Twenty-Four

Sal Hernandez was aware the Hurricane would make landfall during the night. He did not know how fast the flood waters were rising. Electricity was sporadic, but he did receive an updated weather report showing the massive size of Hurricane Harvey.

Unknown to him, water covered his street, his lawn, and crept inside the first floor of his home. During the early morning hours he awoke to an eerie silence. No sounds of traffic racing over highways, no sirens blaring, no teenagers driving by with loud music.

Alarmed, he sprang from the bed. His feet hit the floor, and he felt the cool sensation of water above his ankles. Reaching out in the pitch-black darkness, he was thankful the power company must have turned off the electricity to his neighborhood.

An inventory of food in his refrigerator and freezer flashed through his mind. His plan had been to cook today and warm left overs in the microwave in the coming days.

"Food keeps for three days if you don't open the door." He mumbled, and jammed his foot into something sharp and metal. He felt a sudden burning pain shoot from the jagged cut as he grabbed the flashlight from the top of the dresser. Light flooded the area. He spotted blood oozing from his toe, and tended to the laceration. Gently slipping the boots on, he focused on their height.

Five more inches, and water would be over them. Hurrying about the house, he gathered his cell phone, rifle, ammunition, and a backpack of survival items. He placed all of it on the stairs leading to the second floor of the two story home. Water continued rising at a faster pace.

At first it was only one foot inside the house, then two feet. He carried his stash of survival items higher up the stairs. After a few hours, he moved them to an upstairs bedroom near a window. He discovered another flashlight, and decided to save both for later use. He sat in the dark by the window waiting for daybreak to appear. Water was half-way up the stairs when Sal thought he heard a strange banging outside.

"Maybe something floating inside hit against the wall?" He muttered to himself, and heard the banging sound again. "But there are no waves in the water."

In that instant, glass shattered from a bedroom down the hall. Sal grabbed his rifle.

Looters.

Standing at the side of the window, he stared out at the shadowy image of someone in a boat climbing into his other window.

"Halt, or I'll shoot," Sal hollered.

A shot was fired at the man entering the window, and Sal hadn't had time to take aim. His mind whirled at the thought of someone else outside with a gun.

Who is protecting my property?

He ran down the hall to the next bedroom and looked out the shattered window. Without much moonlight, he could still make out the tops of houses surrounded by the moving flood waters.

A mosquito whined near his head, and he slapped at it absentmindedly.

Sal looked at the man below, bent over in the boat, moaning.

"May God have mercy on your soul," Sal shouted.

The man sluggishly raised his head and gazed into Sal's eyes, then slowly looked down at his fresh new wound. The blood started to drain from it, and Sal could see the pain and sting the man felt through the expression he made. The man thought back to the preacher he had heard on the radio and stopped. He tried putting other thoughts together. Bleeding a tremendous amount of blood, he could feel death's cold grip ease onto him like a winter's chill. Fear. Overwhelming fear. His eyes started to water, and he shut them tightly; mumbling the only thing he could think of to save himself, "Lord, forgive me. Please…"

Sal heard him, and leaning out the window noticed another boat a few houses down. It slipped through the shadows and disappeared.

"Must have been vigilantes." Sal spoke to the intruder, but the man didn't reply. He slumped to the bottom of the boat, and remained lifeless.

Sal called 911, but couldn't get through.

He had no way of knowing officials were receiving 56,000 calls at the Houston area 911 call center. Normally, they receive 8,000 in the same time period.

Remembering Lavinia had a detective friend, Sal phoned her requesting help, but she didn't answer. With his signal breaking up, he left her a message, and hoped for the best.

At daybreak, Sal noticed many items in the boat the intruder must had stolen from other homes. Four television sets, and several jewelry cases littered the boat. The man hadn't moved.

Hours later, a uniformed police officer, and an EMS worker arrived in a rescue boat. After getting information from Sal, they decided to take the man away by pulling the boat behind theirs. The man was deceased. A positive ID was made on the intruder. Richard

Moore wouldn't be bothering anyone again, and his last words were spoken in earnest.

Sal used one of the first responders phones to call Lavinia. He gave her the news about Richard Moore being identified. Sal left with the rescue boat, and was taken to a hospital for a possible staph infection.

Chapter Twenty-Five

Caddo Lake State Park, one of many Texas state parks offering shelter to refugees, quickly filled all of their cabins. Days passed as frantic calls went out searching for other friends and relatives left behind. Videos shown on television and social media were shocking and difficult to watch. Massive flooding brought horrific emergency conditions as cars went underwater and people were plucked from rooftops, and trees amid swirling, rising water. Shelters were packed beyond capacity.

Ethan, Kate, Maria, Carlos and Rosa sat in the Ranger's Station with other refugees watching the digital television mounted on the wall. Each day they absorbed everything related to south Texas and Louisiana; viewing the storms aftermath of destruction.

Kate finally had to turn away from the television. It was too painful to watch. Too many memories flooded back in her mind of the other hurricane, Hurricane Katrina, and the changing effects it had on her own life. Her heart had gone out to those victims. Now her heart went out to all the victims of this hurricane, Hurricane Harvey. Kate knew first hand that it was too soon for these victims to realize the true extent of damage. What they saw barely touched the surface.

Quietly leaving the group, she made her way to a huge display of a hollow cypress tree. Kate bent over, entered and stood inside the tree. Carlos and Rosa ran and joined her, suddenly having something to laugh about.

"We're in a tree." Their young voices announced with joy. Running their small hands over the smooth wood, they giggled.

Maria and Ethan heard the laughter, and hastened to the tree display.

"Life goes on." Maria said.

"Yes, it does, and I think it's time for a wedding." Ethan raised his eyebrows at Kate.

"Here?"

"Maybe. It's up to you. We can go to the courthouse in Marshall, and get a marriage license. Start the ball rolling."

Kate stepped out of the tree grabbing Ethan's extended hand.

For the first time in days, Kate experienced a warm, pleasant feeling. "Maria, take my place. We'll be back soon."

Ethan and Kate left and finally located the courthouse in Marshall. He paid for the marriage license, and they toured the museum in the old, historic courthouse on the town square. Build in 1900; it was restored, and indeed a beautiful, impressive structure.

They drove a few blocks to the boarding kennel to play with Rufus. The little dog jumped and barked wildly at the sight of them. They each hugged him, and Rufus wanted to play. He ran to his bed and brought his ball to Ethan.

"He loves this Kate. Watch him chase the ball, then tease me hiding with it." He threw the ball to the dog, and

228

Rufus scampered over the slick, tiled floor retrieving it. He held it in his mouth and quickly ran off hiding behind a filing cabinet.

"Come on out, Rufus." Ethan grinned. "Come here, little guy."

Rufus darted out and dropped the ball in Ethan's hand.

"Good boy."

Kate snatched the dog into her arms. "Aren't you a smart one?" She hugged him and rubbed the back of his ears. Rufus jumped and licked her cheek.

Glancing at Ethan, she noticed him staring off into the distance.

"Hey, you okay?"

"Yeah. I hadn't thought of Becky in a while. Until now."

He strolled toward Kate and patted Rufus. The dog wiggled in Kate's arms, and he darted back to her face with another lick.

"Becky never had anything to do with Rufus. Why she took him with her when she left, I do not know."

"Maybe to bark? Maybe she took him as a watch dog?"

"Steve had a dog. I'm sure it barked. Becky didn't always think things through."

"At least you have him back."

Ethan smiled. "Thanks to you."

An hour later, all three were exhausted. Rufus went to his kennel, pawed at the door that was open by an inch, and kept pawing at it until it swung open. He rushed inside his home, and curled into his blanket.

"Time to go." Ethan reached inside and patted the dog. Stopping at the main desk on their way out, Ethan waited to pay for the past weeks boarding, and for an additional week.

The owner looked appalled.

"Oh no. This is on me. I insist."

Ethan and Kate exchanged a glance of wide- eyed wonder.

"Thank you, ma'am." Ethan shook her hand.

"Yes, thank you for your kindness." Kate added.

"It's the least I can do. Go on, now, before we start getting emotional."

They left waving by to her and returned to the car.

"Sure wasn't expecting that." Ethan turned to Kate and gave a slight smile.

"Me either. That was nice."

He started the car, and turned to Kate again.

"Let's find a gas station and fill up before heading back to the park. We can think about eating then. Maybe take Maria and the kids sightseeing today or tomorrow."

"Sounds good to me. They'll like getting out."

Returning to the park, they noticed over ten cars parked around the Ranger's Station. Many people were walking around outside.

After the time they'd spent together at the park, the refugees were like family, but neither Kate nor Ethan recognized any from this group.

They drove to the cabins, and parked.

Maria and her children burst out the door of their cabin and ran to the car.

"Guess what has happened?" Maria's eyes sparkled and without waiting for their response, her bubbly voice continued. "The local churches and restaurants in Karnack brought food for everyone here at the park. They wanted to help the refugees."

"A lot of people are helping." Ethan and Kate exited the car appearing dazed again. He looked at Maria. "The owner at the boarding kennel in Marshall wouldn't let us pay for boarding Rufus."

Maria shook her head at Ethan. "This is such a caring community. And some even brought toys and their own children to play with the kids staying here at the park."

Kate beamed. "It's a blessing."

Chapter Twenty-Six

Kate and Ethan married the following week. The ceremony, officiated by a local pastor, was held at Caddo Lake State Park. They were surrounded by their new family of refugees. Rosa loved being the flower girl. She skipped around throwing flowers, and then she'd stop and curtsy at random, smiling broadly. Maria was the Matron of Honor, and Carlos had a dual role. He walked Kate down the aisle, and gave her away. Then Carlos stood next to Ethan as his best man. Carlos was ecstatic, and later told everyone he was now a man.

Ethan called Pastor Williford often, checking on him. Kate kept in touch with Lavinia through the entire time they had left Houston, and of course Maria and her husband, Sal, called each other daily. After much discussion, it was decided for the small group of neighbors to return to Houston.

Mixed feelings were obvious, and prayers were spoken for safe travel.

They packed, said their goodbyes, and picked Rufus up in Marshall.

In five hours, they would arrive back home.

Chapter Twenty-Seven

"Lavinia, we're on the road."

"I can't wait to see all of you. Kate, I feel like my family is coming."

"We are family. I think us neighbors have a stronger bond than some real families have."

"Remember what Pastor Williford told us about unity?"

"Yes. He said we were in unity with Christ. That's our bond, Lavinia."

"Yes, and it's a strong bond. I couldn't have made it this far without it."

"Same here. We'll be in Jacksonville in an hour and a half."

"I'm packed, and ready to go. See you soon."

"By." Kate ended the call, and considered her husband.

"Ethan, thanks for planning on stopping in Jacksonville to bring Lavinia with us."

"Well, she has to feel lost living with Ben's relatives, I mean; she's never met them before, has she?"

"No, and she's been there two weeks, now. Seems like we've been gone longer than two weeks."

"Two weeks away from home is long enough. The water should be receding." He hesitated, and rubbed his jaw. "Does Ben know we're bringing her to Houston?"

"No, she's surprising him. He has no idea we're stopping to get her."

"Well, it's on the way. We go directly through Jacksonville."

Maria sat in the back seat listening, and suddenly tapped Ethan on his shoulder. "What if the water hasn't receded?"

"Some places do still have a lot of water. It rained 51 inches in some areas in just under five days, but Sal and Pastor Williford told me this morning we should be able to drive to their shelter."

"I hope so." She leaned back in the seat. "And I'm thankful Sal didn't get a staph infection. He could still be in a hospital somewhere."

Carlos and Rosa chatted with excitement among themselves. They were too young to notice the concerned looks on the adults as their silence grew. Kate recognized the quietness. She handed Rufus to the children hoping their squeals of enjoyment would drown out any worries plaguing the adults.

Arriving in Jacksonville seemed to take no time at all. Everyone exited the car, and met Ben Marino's sister-in-law. Ben's brother was at work. After a cordial greeting, and quick goodbyes, they returned to the car, making room for Lavinia and her few belongings. She sat in the front seat next to Kate, and her luggage and totes were placed on top of the already high pile in the back.

"Have you heard from your parents?"

Lavinia winced at Kate. "My parents had to move in with my sister in Brenham. They said it's hard to locate their friends."

"So much sorrow..."

Ethan interrupted. "Have you heard from Ben lately?"

"Yes. Yesterday he admitted he's working twelve hour shifts with only one day off a week. He said he feels guilty taking that one day off. They still receive an excessive amount of calls for help."

"It doesn't sound like the situation is improving. No one can work if it's that bad. There will be no jobs. No place to stay." Maria voiced her opinion, and Kate turned to see her absentmindedly wringing her hands.

"We'll be okay. We can start over." Kate spoke in a warm, caring tone.

"If that's the case, then we'll pick up Sal, and be on our way. Don't fret, Maria." Ethan looked at her again in his rear view mirror. "We can always go to Kansas. I still have my parents' old farm house there."

"You are a kind man, Ethan."

Silence returned and seemed to have a calming effect on everyone. The children napped, and soon the little dog curled against them, also falling to sleep.

As they approached Houston a few hours later each adult stared out the car windows; alert and anxious.

Detour signs were numerous. Flood waters still covering some highways and exits were mind-boggling. No one spoke as Ethan made his way to the shelter. In the midst of destruction, they spotted the Texas Baptist Disaster Relief Team trucks; all volunteers helping muck-out homes, and feed thousands. Ethan kept driving and winding through neighborhoods in the detour. Another volunteer group, Samaritan's Purse, had arrived. Also handing out food, and supplies to thousands; both organizations were a blessing to all. Many other organizations arrived that same day to help.

Ruined furniture, wet carpet, molded sheet-rock, and muddy clothes were piled on sidewalks. The stench of rotten food hung in the air from freezers and refrigerators that were tossed in the piles for removal.

Ethan finally arrived at the shelter, and noticed the Red Cross trucks parked in front.

"Wait in the car. I'll try and find Sal and Pastor Williford." He rushed off.

Entering the tent at the entrance of the shelter; he spoke to a Red Cross representative.

Fifteen minutes later, he returned with Sal, Pastor Williford with his walking cane, and an assortment of tote-bags, and luggage. Everyone hurried from the car. Maria was first to hug her husband, followed by their children. Kate and Lavinia gave the Pastor a group hug.

"Sal, put your stuff in the back." Ethan opened the car door, and Sal grabbed two of three extra large tote-bags.

Kate looked alarmed at the Pastor. "Aren't you coming with us? You aren't staying here are you?"

"No, they'll have to close the shelter soon, and relocate everyone. Our neighborhood had over twelve feet of water. Nothing will be normal here for a long time. No place to stay. No jobs."

"We were afraid of that. Pastor, you can come with us." Ethan offered, and glanced at Sal. "Looks like we're going to Kansas. I have my parents' old farm house there. We can all start over."

"Much obliged, Ethan." Sal embraced him, and quickly stepped back. "I can't thank you enough."

"Pastor?" Ethan glanced at the older man.

"It's a good time for a vacation. My daughter in New Mexico has been after me to visit. I'm taking a train. Looking forwards to the ride, and scenery, and of course the visit."

"Well, you know you're welcome. I wasn't expecting to see this much destruction, Pastor. I thought we could move back."

"No, Ethan. Most people won't be moving back. Many have no flood insurance. I found out FEMA will offer the victims a low interest rate loan to rebuild, but no one I talked to can afford to take on another debt. If you're making a car payment and can't drive it, and make a house payment and can't live in it; you sure can't pay back a loan to FEMA."

"That's true. I know I can't. I have to walk away from my home." Kate sighed.

"Same here." Sal nodded.

"At my age, I couldn't rebuild if I wanted to. Material and labor costs are too high. Can't afford it, but I'm thankful for that old farmhouse." Ethan smiled.

"And thankful we are all here." Pastor Williford hesitated. "One of our church members didn't make it, T9C Star died." He looked at Lavinia. "That was the stepmother of the little girl that sang solos in our church. She was Daniel Star's new wife."

"How horrible." Kate whispered. "How sad for all of them."

Pastor Williford nodded. "Last I heard 47 deaths occurred. We have to keep praying for everyone, and move forward. Lavinia, Sal told me about Richard. Thank God he asked for forgiveness before he died. Always pray for your enemies to know Jesus Christ as their Savior. Have you talked to Ben?"

"No, but I'm going to call him. He'll be surprised I'm here."

She slipped away from the group and called Ben Marino.

He answered on the third ring.
"Hello?"

"Ben, it's me, Lavinia. Guess what? I'm here in Houston."

"What? What happened? I thought you were still at my brother's house."

"I wanted to surprise you. I caught a ride with my neighbors."

"Oh. Lavinia, it's a mess here. I'm working day and night, and we aren't anywhere close to catching up. Are you going to your parents' house?"

"I...I could. They do need help."

"Well, keep in touch. Sorry I can't see you now."

"That's okay, I understand."

"Well, I have to run."

"Take care."

"You too, by."

"By."

One tear fell, and Lavinia rubbed her eyes. Refusing to cry, she walked back to the group. "You know what? I love you guys. I really do. You are my special church family, my neighbors."

Kate approached her slowly. "And we love you. Is he coming out here to see you?"

"No. He mentioned something about going to my parents' house. I didn't tell him it wasn't livable. He doesn't know they are in Brenham at my sister's."

Pastor Williford walked to her. "Lavinia, he has a commitment to his job. He'd work 24 hours a day, 7 days a week if he could, simply to help. Do you want to stay with your parents, or go on to Kansas?"

"I want to help my parents."

"Okay, then get your things out of the car. You can ride the train with me. It goes right through Brenham."

"Thanks." She said, sounding anxious. "But how...?"

He faced the group and triumph gleamed in his eyes. "Everything has a way of working out when it's God's will. One of the Texas Baptist men from the Disaster Team is taking me to the train station. He should be here in about five minutes." He glanced at Lavinia, and spoke in a quiet voice. "Do you need help buying a train ticket?"

"No, Ben suggested I sell my car, and I did. I have cash; a lot of cash."

A truck arrived with the words 'Texas Baptist Disaster Relief Team' on the side. Pastor Williford made his way to the driver and shook his hand, talking non-stop as they loaded his and Lavinia's bags and luggage.

Hugs were given, and goodbyes were said. Within seconds, the yellow and blue truck raced away.

Kate stood alone, watching the truck disappear around a curve. She felt someone's arm circle her waist. Ethan's presence overwhelmed her. Struggling to speak, she uttered, "There goes part of my heart."

Ethan gently gave her a hug.
"They'll always be part of our lives.
And remember, God has a plan for all of
us. He's sending them where they are
needed, and us too."

He turned to the Hernandez
family. "Ready for Kansas?"

Carlos raised his hand. "I am."

Rosa thrust her tiny hand in the
air. "Me too, I'm ready."

Sal tipped his head back and
closed his eyes. He mumbled a short
prayer.

Maria, her face radiant, replied,
"Lead the way."

To be continued...
In Book Three, "Mind of a
Neighbor" of the American
Neighborhood Series.

About the author…

Lynn Hobbs is a member of the American Christian Fiction Writers, Jerry Jenkins Writers Guild, Pulpwood Queens Book Club, Rave Writers International Society of Authors, Rave Reviews Book Club, Texas Association of Authors, a lifetime member of World Wide Who's Who, and is a Southern Baptist.

Author of the award-winning Running Forward Series, and Christian Biography:

Book one, Sin, Secrets, and Salvation; awarded 1st Place, Religious Fiction,

2013, by the Texas Association of Authors.

Book two, River Town; awarded 1st Place, Religious Fiction, 2014, by the Texas Association of Authors.

Book three, Hidden Creek; awarded 1st Place, Religious Fiction, 2015, by the Texas Association of Authors.

Lillie, A Motherless Child, {Christian Biography} awarded 1st Place, Biography, 2016, by the Texas Association of Authors.

The American Neighborhood Series
{Christian Fiction}

Book one of three, Eyes of a Neighbor, published 12-11-2016.

All books are available on Amazon.com

Mrs. Hobbs loves to hear from her readers. Please contact her at lynnhobbs.author@gmail.com

And visit her website at www.LynnHobbsAuthor.com

All reviews on Amazon appreciated!

Eyes of a Neighbor
by Lynn Hobbs

"Eyes of a Neighbor" is book one of
Lynn Hobbs new Christian Fiction American
Neighborhood Series. Meet the neighbors,
both old and new, set in a gated community in
the older, historic section of Houston, Texas.
Targeted recently by the criminal element,
turmoil increases. Based on the author's own
knowledge of having once lived in the
Heights area, the residents created include all

age groups who become tangled in a murder mystery. Romance, suspense, intrigue, and inspiration, intertwine to offer a fast paced read that is indeed a page turner. Who can new resident Kate Davis trust? Has she chosen the wrong friends? Can the neighbors trust her?

Readers can expect to find real life situations that will be surprising.

Large print paperback, regular print Kindle. No profanity. No graphic violence.

Book three in the series, Mind of a Neighbor, available in 2018, will conclude the series.

A Motherless Child
By: Lynn Hobbs

The true life story of Lillie Fritsche. One of sixteen siblings, born in the depression era. Lillie's mother passed away when she was seven years old. Follow her journey from a motherless child to an inspiring woman of faith.

A word from the publisher:

LIKE THE BOOK?

HELP THE AUTHOR!

REVIEWS HELP WITH FUTURE
SALES

GIVE A REVIEW ON
AMAZON.COM

Did you know? Authors are not rich. In fact, most make less than $10,000. a year. Being an author is small business.

If there are 50 reviews, amazon lists a book in its newsletters and other promotions. (Also boughts.)

REVIEWS are the easiest way to say THANK YOU to the author and tell their publisher to produce more books.

SUPPORT AUTHORS

SUPPORT SMALL BUSINESS

What to do!

1. GO TO AMAZON.COM

2. IN THE LONG, BLANK SEARCH WINDOW AT TOP OF PAGE, LEFT HAND CORNER; TYPE IN BOOK TITLE, A COMMA, AND AUTHOR NAME. EXAMPLE: RIVER TOWN, LYNN HOBBS

3. CLICK ON THE BOOK TITLE

4. CLICK ON THE HYPERLINK THAT SAYS... CUSTOMER REVIEWS.

5. THEN CLICK ON THE HYPERLINK THAT SAYS...WRITE A CUSTOMER REVIEW

6. CLICK ON THE NUMBER OF STARS YOU WANT TO GIVE (5 ARE BEST)

7. TYPE IN THE COMMENT AREA TO WRITE YOUR REVIEW: THEY CAN BE SHORT, FOR EXAMPLE…"I LIKE IT." IT'S THE NUMBER OF REVIEWS THAT MATTERS MOST.

A GOOD REVIEW IS LIKE GOLD TO AN AUTHOR. IF YOU HAVE EVER BOUGHT ANYTHING ON AMAZON, YOU AUTOMATICALLY HAVE AN ACCOUNT, AND CAN WRITE A REVIEW. REVIEWS ARE SINCERELY APPRICIATED!

THANK YOU!

On the next few pages, check out some more great books from the publisher!

The Nephilim, A Giant Walk Through History
By: Jeff E. Brannon

A Biblically based, mostly historic, fictional story starting from the time of Jared (Noah's grandfather) through the present day. The word Nephilim is translated in Gen 6:1 as giant, but means "from the fallen ones". They were the offspring from the Fallen Angels and the daughters of Adam. It is an exciting adventure filled with historical content designed to be a springboard for the reader to explore a side of history often not told. I believe one cannot fully comprehend the Old Testament without understanding the role the Nephilim played. This book helps answer questions like, "If God is a God of love, why did He allow genocide in the OT?" and "What did Jesus mean that the last days would be like the days of Noah?" The book pulls from Ancient Biblical text as well as scrolls found along the Dead Sea Scrolls such as The Book of Giants. The synchronized, Biblically endorsed, extra-Biblical texts such as 1 Enoch, Jasher, and Jubilees also contribute to the historical accuracy of the narrative. Find out about the Vimana mentioned in over 1,000 text in ancient writings and how they tie in with the Nephilim and Watcher-class angels. This book answers questions the modern church typically runs from in an exciting story-driven narrative that puts the reader right in the middle of the action. In this story, the author takes you on a journey from the dawn of time through the present day and even portrays a glimpse in what might happen in the very near future. Who were Nimrod and his wife? How do they tie in to events both in the past and the future? Who are the Nephilim? Are they real? Do they live among us? Find out the answers to these and many more questions in this book today.

"Something extraordinary has happened. Due to a happy accident with our logistics division we have been handed an opportunity to push the boundaries on a global stage." Leon replied without looking from the screen. "So we are training them to be soldiers?" "No, no. We don't need more soldiers. We need something better. We have a chance to eliminate the need for war all together. When you control the monster, what is there left to fear?" On a fateful fall day in Texas, Luke Jones is stabbed, burned, and left for dead while, in a nearby city, Francis Guy is mugged, bludgeoned and left to the same fate. They awaken, not only alive and fully healed, but captured by an indomitable government agency. There, Jones and Guy discover they have been gifted with super-human like abilities as they are forced to undergo one life threatening trial after another. With only each other for support, Jones and Guy become a formidable team as they are pitted against others with abilities beyond imagination. When faced with a grim ultimatum, they perform a daring escape back into the free world, leaving smoke and bodies in their wake. With nowhere to run and their very lives at stake, the duo split up in an attempt to take down this ruthless organization with the very same powers they were being trained to use. Thrown into a series of extraordinary circumstances, they meet both friend and foe alike as the battles they waged in captivity prove more and more useful. Will they drown under a sea of government conspiracy or will they rise from the ashes of their former lives and be reborn?

266